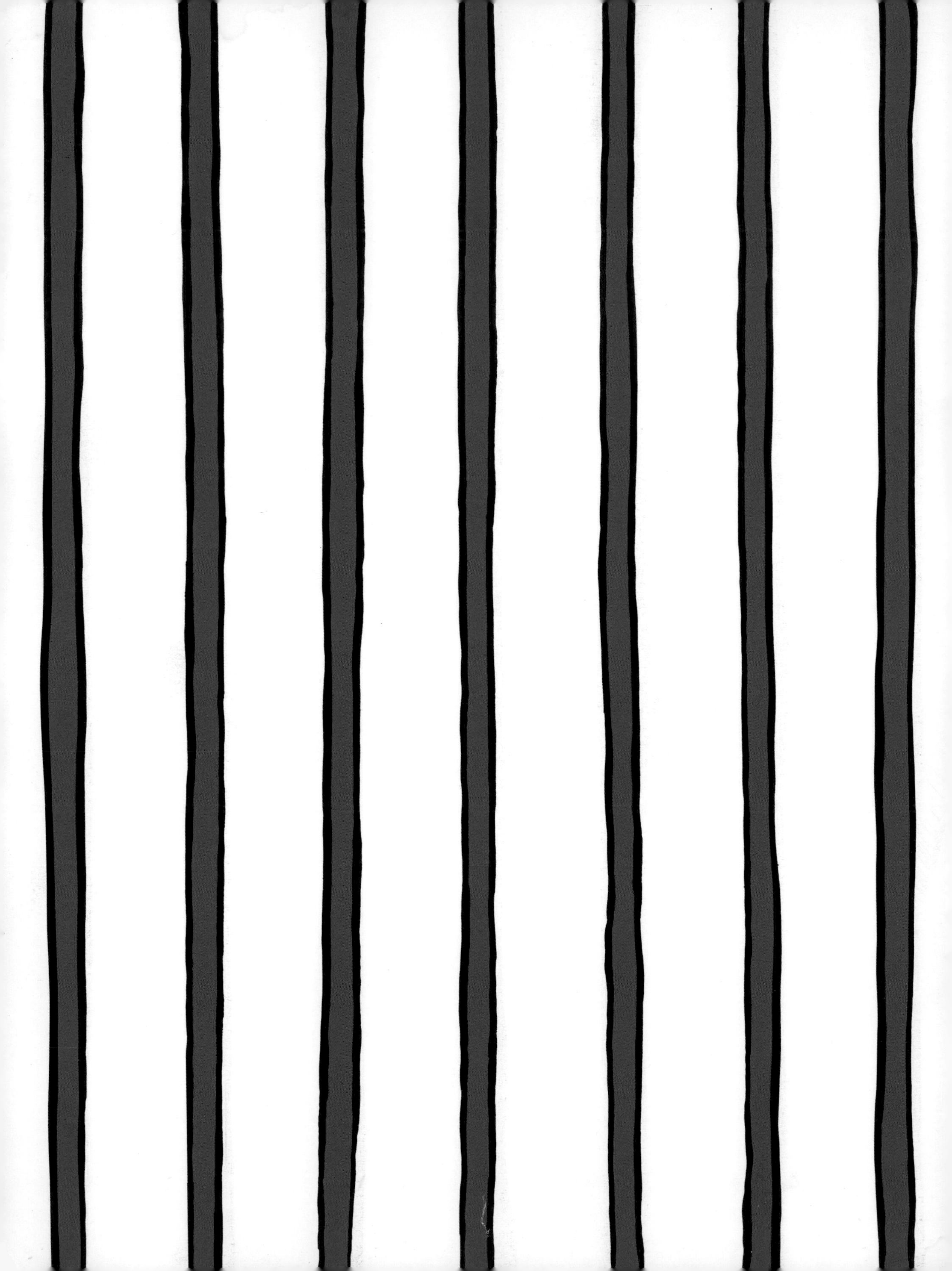

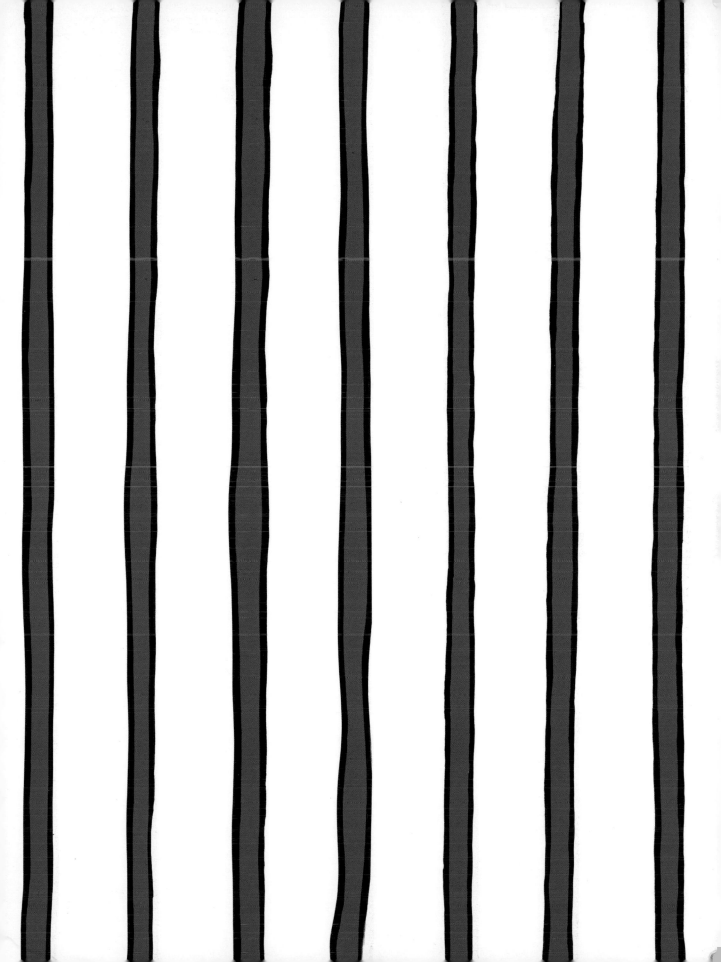

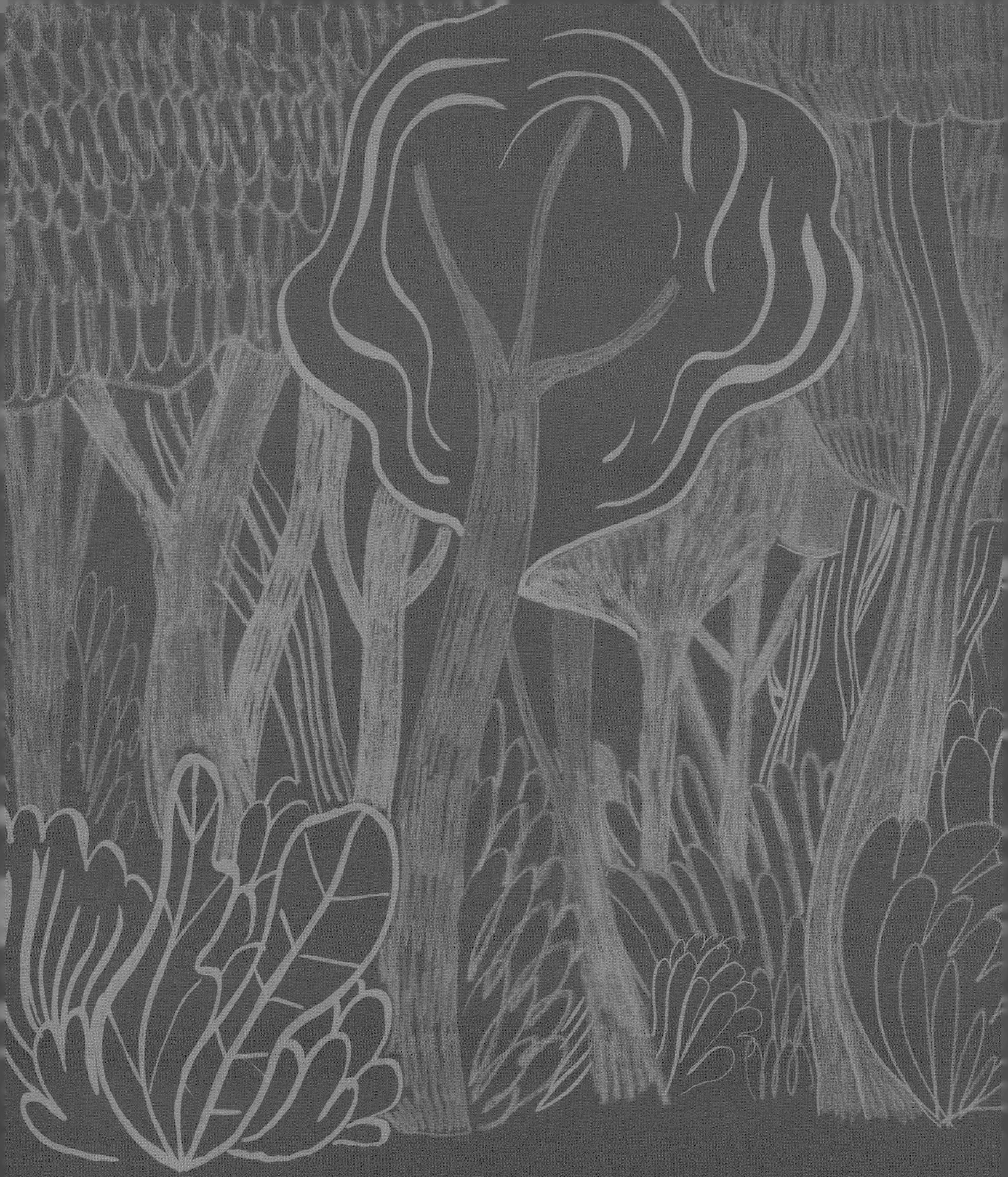

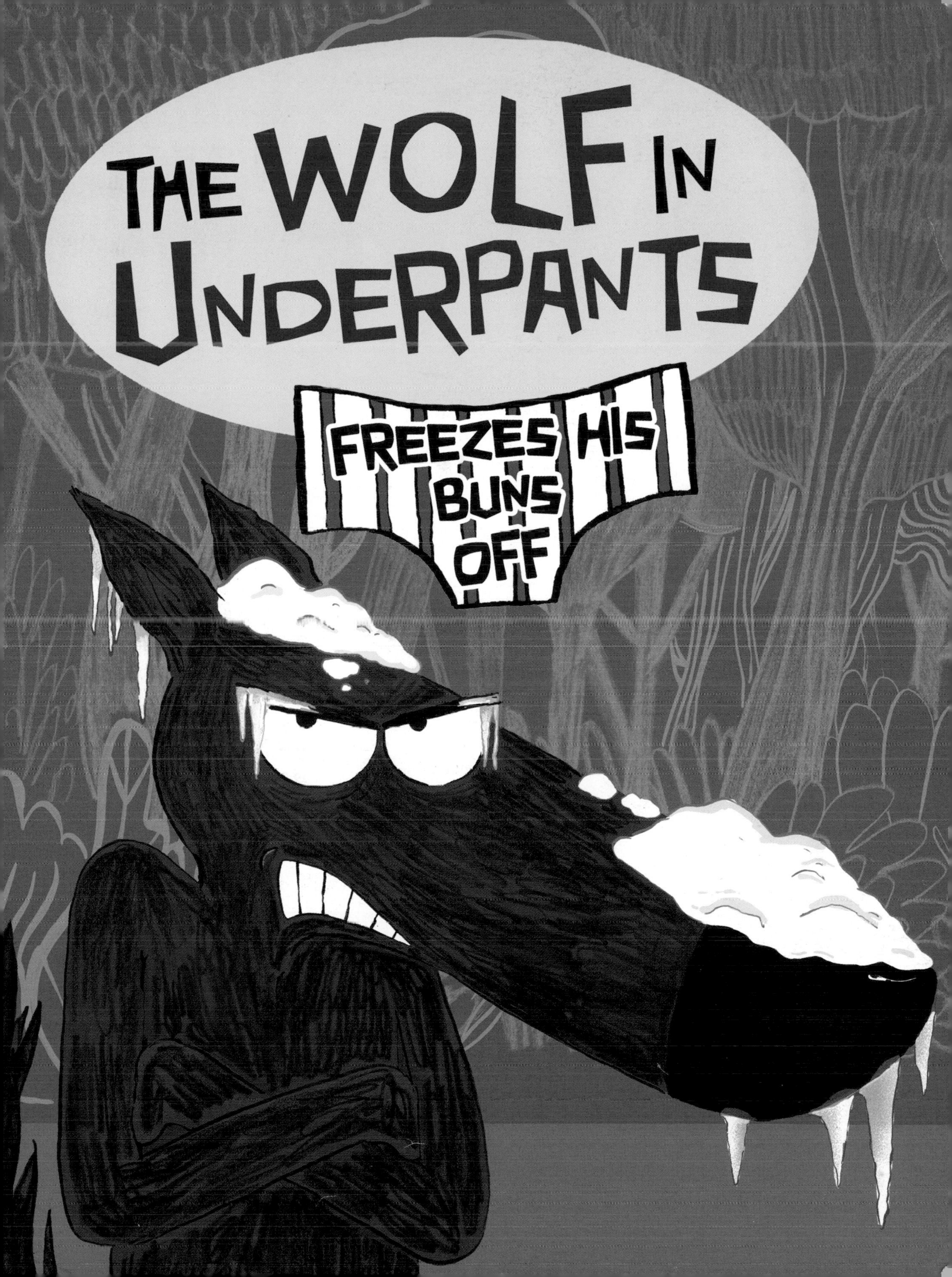
THE WOLF IN UNDERPANTS
FREEZES HIS BUNS OFF

Story by Wilfrid Lupano
Art by Mayana Itoïz
With the friendly artistic participation of Paul Cauuet
Translation by Nathan Sacks

First American edition published in 2020 by Graphic Universe™
Published by arrangement with Mediatoon Licensing - France
Le Loup en slip se les gèle méchamment
© Dargaud Benelux (Dargaud-Lombard S.A.) 2017—Lupano, Itoïz, and Cauuet. All rights
reserved. Original artistic director: Philippe Ravon.
www.dargaud.com

Graphic Universe™
An imprint of Lerner Publishing Group, Inc.
241 First Avenue North
Minneapolis, MN 55401 USA

For reading levels and more information, look up this title at www.lernerbooks.com.

Main body text set in Stick-A-Round. Typeface provided by Pintassilgoprints.

Library of Congress Cataloging-in-Publication Data

Names: Lupano, Wilfrid, 1971- author. | Itoïz, Mayana, 1978- illustrator. | Cauuet, Paul,
    1980- illustrator. | Sacks, Nathan, translator.
Title: The wolf in underpants freezes his buns off / Wilfrid Lupano ; art by Mayana Itoïz and
    Paul Cauuet ; translation by Nathan Sacks.
Other titles: Loup en slip se les gèle méchamment. English
Description: Minneapolis : Graphic Universe, 2020. | Originally published in French by Dargaud
    Benelux in 2017 under title: Le loup en slip se les gèle méchamment. | Summary: When
    the wolf complains about the freezing-cold winter, the other forest animals fear he will
    return to his wild, evil ways.
Identifiers: LCCN 2019008576 | ISBN 9781541528192 (lb : alk. paper)
Subjects: LCSH: Graphic novels. | CYAC: Graphic novels. | Wolves—Fiction. | Forest animals—
    Fiction. | Winter—Fiction.
Classification: LCC PZ7.7.L86 Wq 2020 | DDC 741.5/973—dc23

LC record available at https://lccn.loc.gov/2019008576

Manufactured in the United States of America
1-44702-35533-8/13/2019

THE WOLF IN UNDERPANTS

FREEZES HIS BUNS OFF

Wilfrid Lupano

Mayana Itoïz
and
Paul Cauuet

Graphic Universe™ • Minneapolis

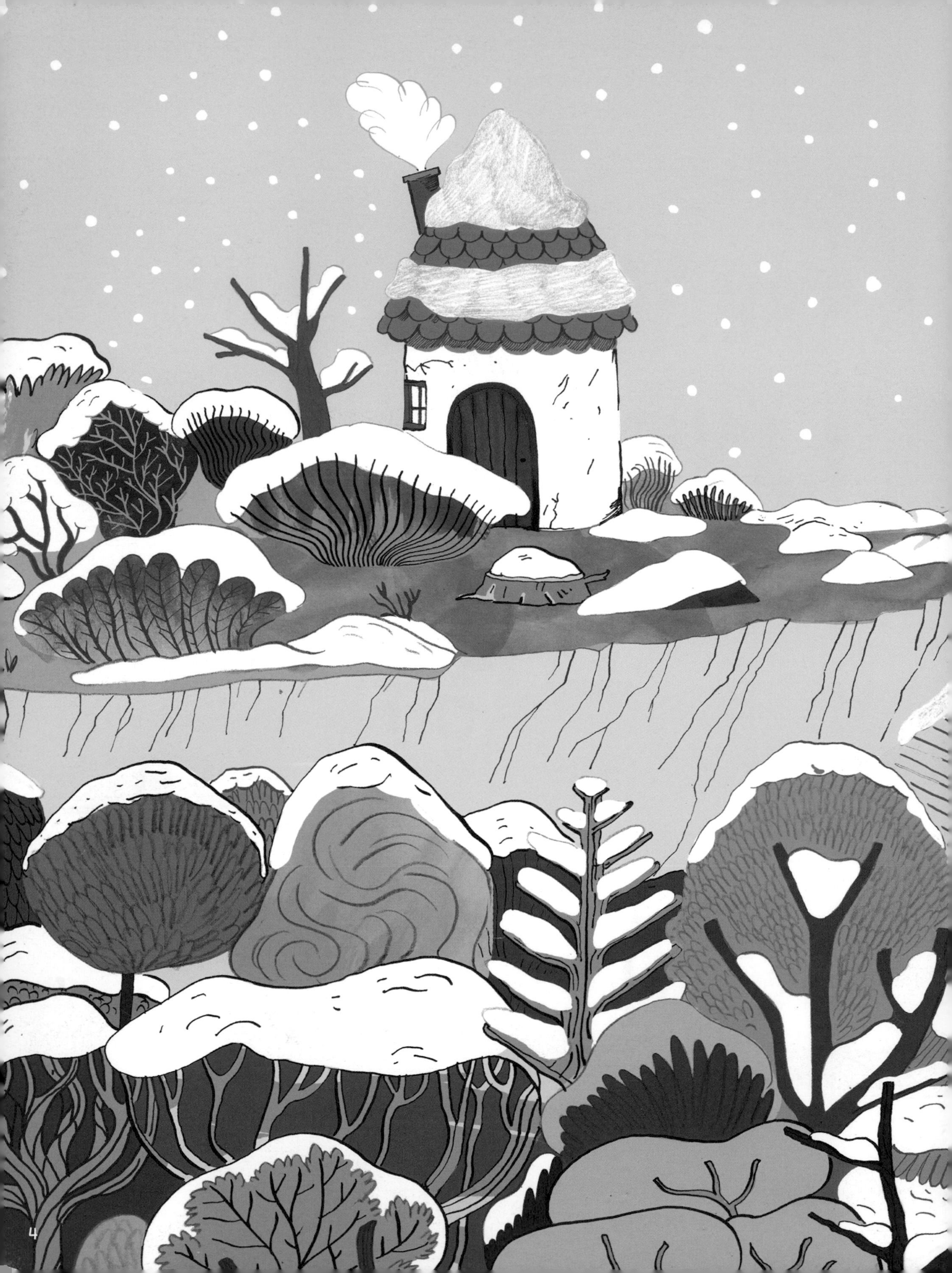

WINTER HAS FALLEN WITHOUT SO MUCH AS A SOUND. AND IN THESE WOODS, WHEN THERE'S SNOW ON THE GROUND, IT GETS COLD AS ALL GET-OUT.

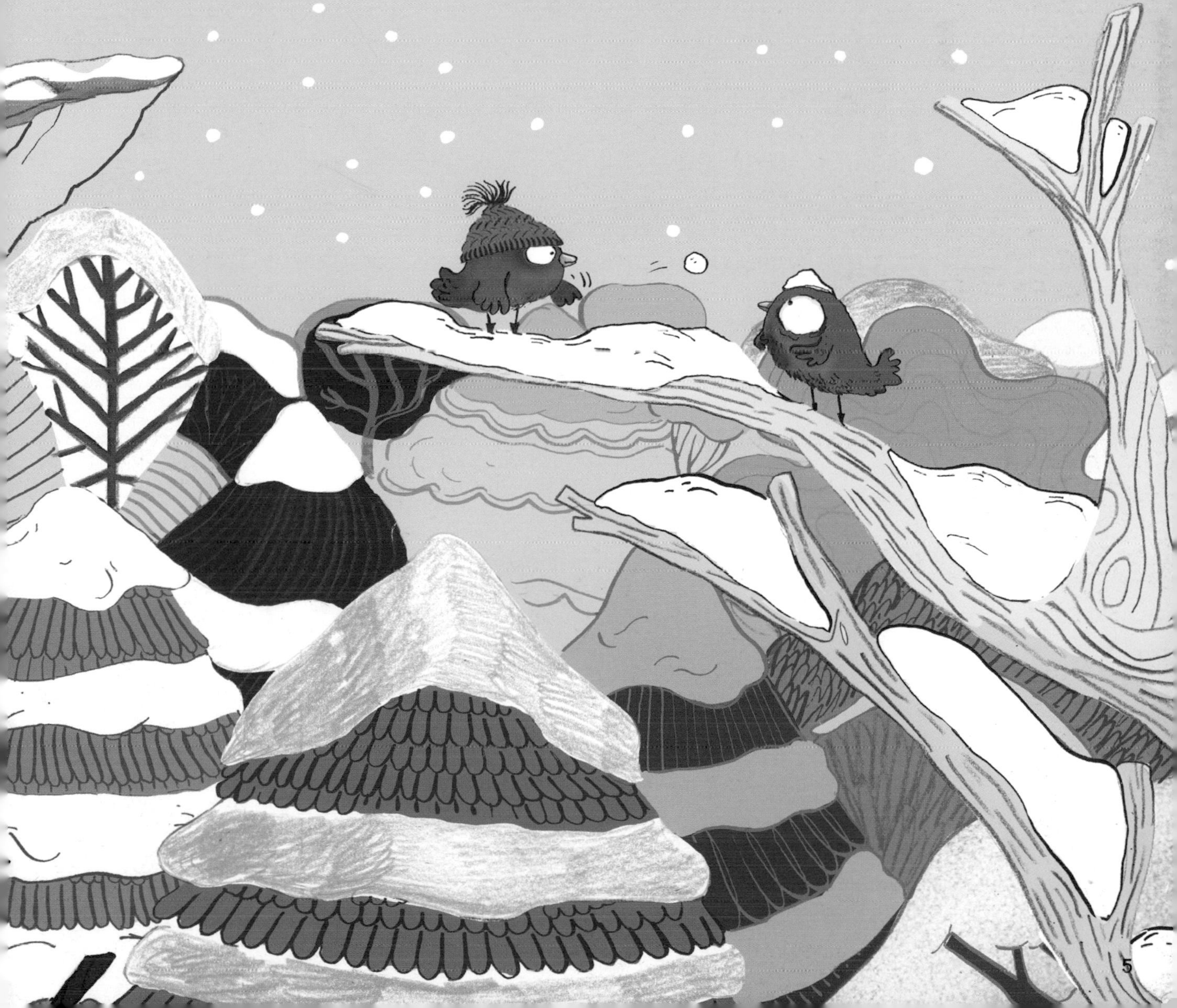

BUT IF YOU'RE PREPARED, WINTER IS NO PROBLEM. IT'S EVEN FUN!

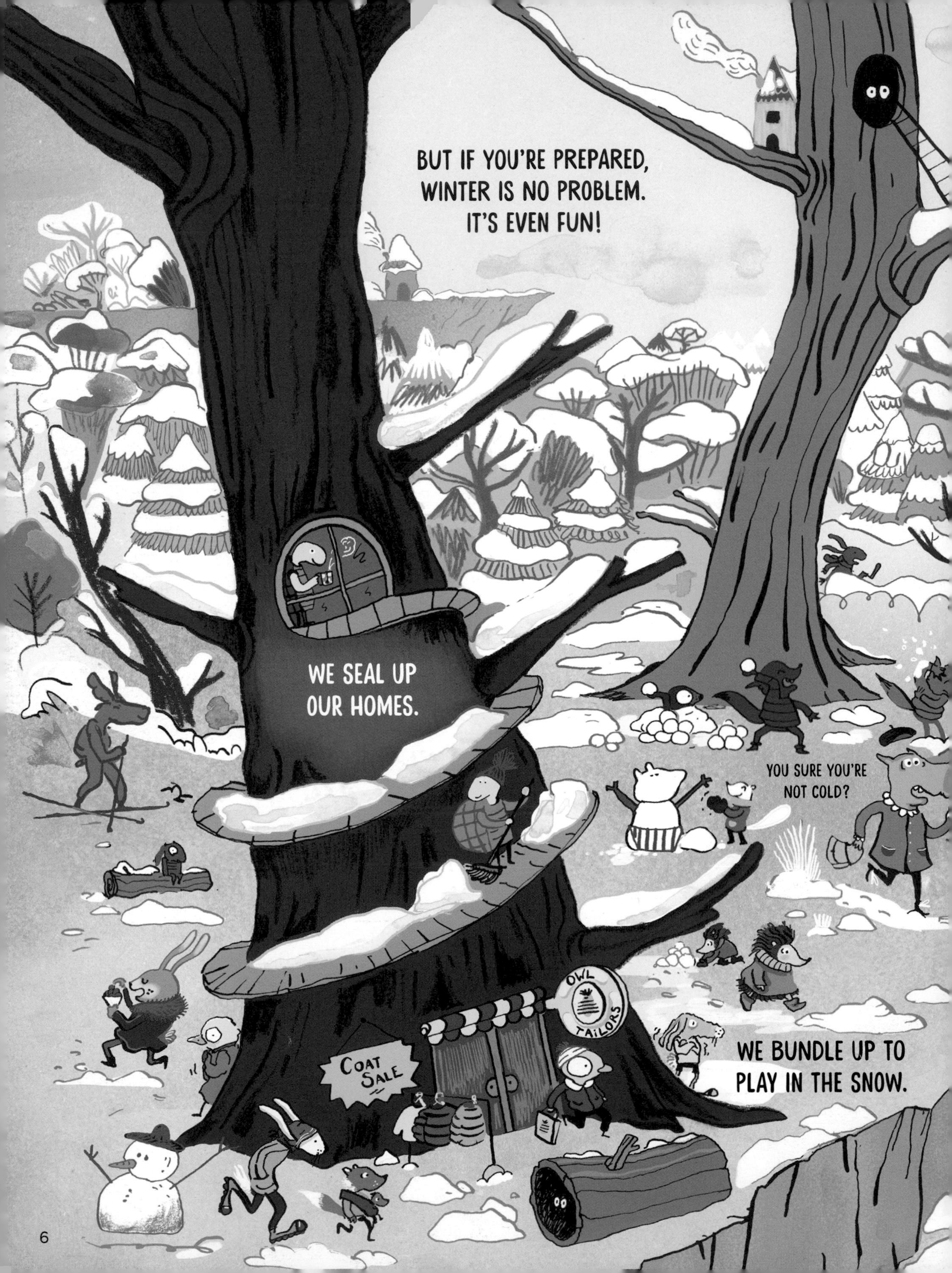
YOU SURE YOU'RE NOT COLD?
COAT SALE
OWL TAILORS

WE SEAL UP OUR HOMES.

WE BUNDLE UP TO PLAY IN THE SNOW.

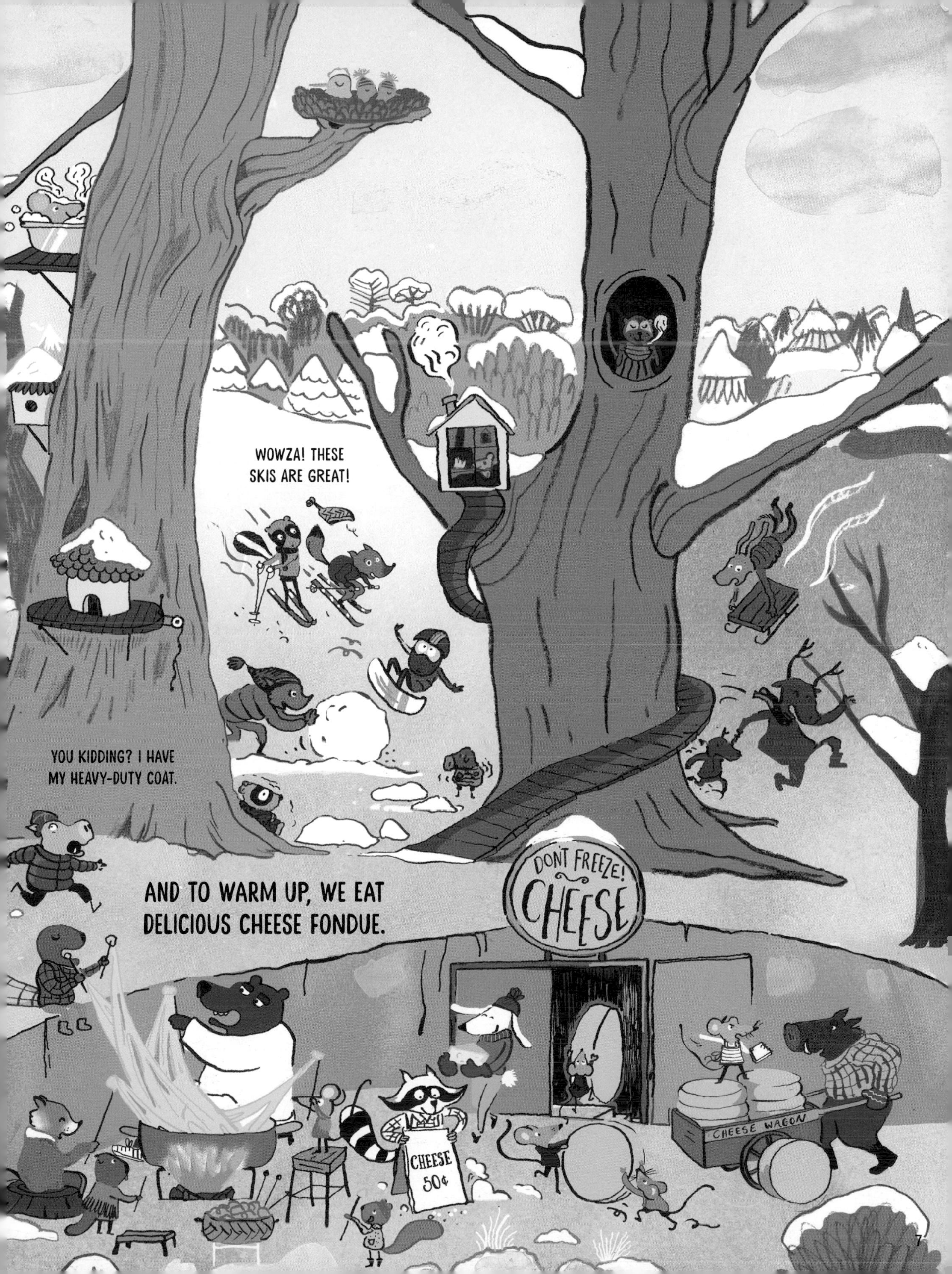
WOWZA! THESE SKIS ARE GREAT!
YOU KIDDING? I HAVE MY HEAVY-DUTY COAT.
DON'T FREEZE! CHEESE
CHEESE 50¢
CHEESE WAGON

AND TO WARM UP, WE EAT DELICIOUS CHEESE FONDUE.

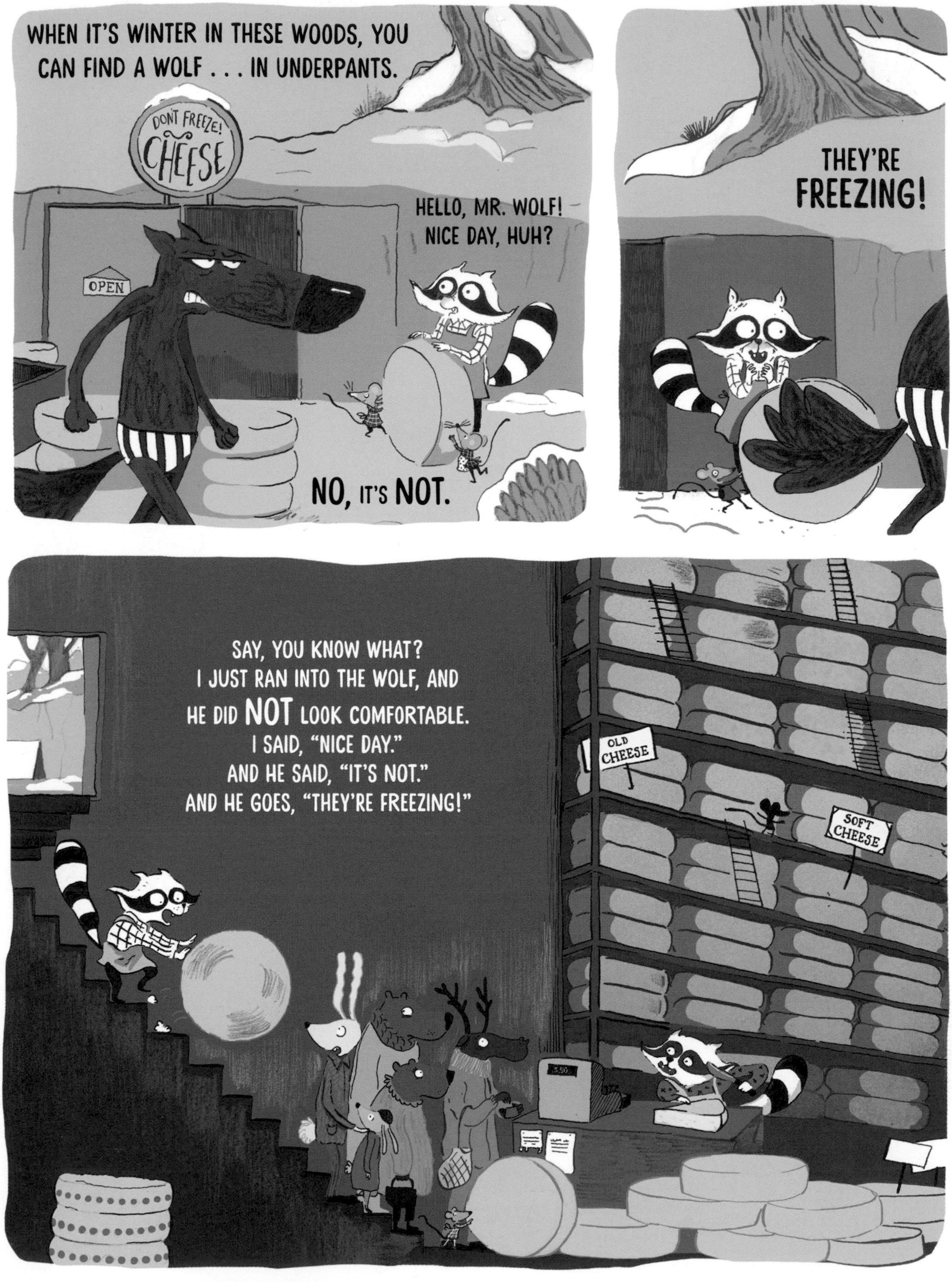
WHEN IT'S WINTER IN THESE WOODS, YOU CAN FIND A WOLF . . . IN UNDERPANTS.
DON'T FREEZE! CHEESE
OPEN
HELLO, MR. WOLF! NICE DAY, HUH?
NO, IT'S NOT.
THEY'RE FREEZING!
SAY, YOU KNOW WHAT? I JUST RAN INTO THE WOLF, AND HE DID NOT LOOK COMFORTABLE. I SAID, "NICE DAY." AND HE SAID, "IT'S NOT." AND HE GOES, "THEY'RE FREEZING!"
OLD CHEESE
SOFT CHEESE

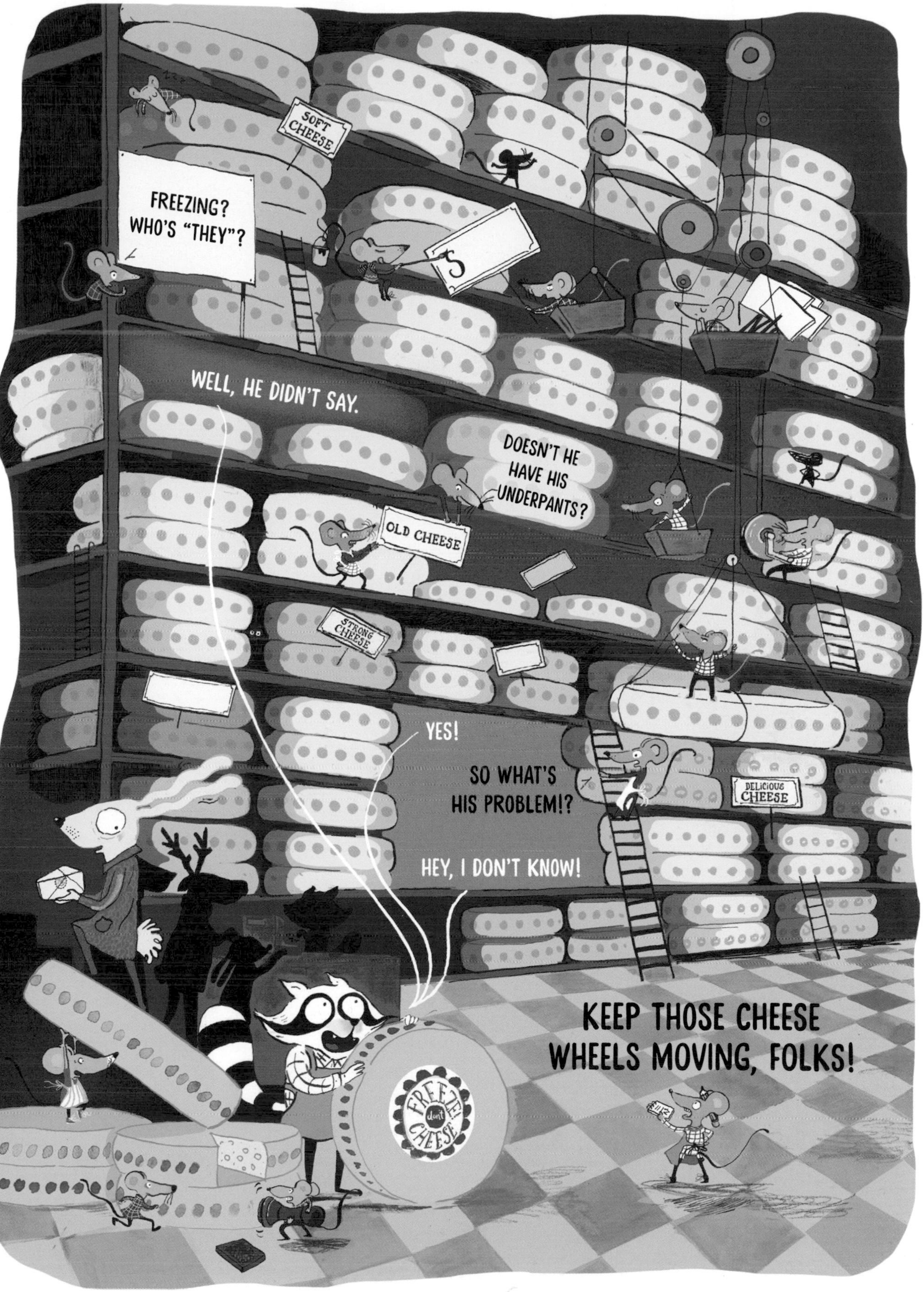

SOFT CHEESE
FREEZING? WHO'S "THEY"?
WELL, HE DIDN'T SAY.
DOESN'T HE HAVE HIS UNDERPANTS?
OLD CHEESE
STRONG CHEESE
YES!
SO WHAT'S HIS PROBLEM!?
DELICIOUS CHEESE
HEY, I DON'T KNOW!
KEEP THOSE CHEESE WHEELS MOVING, FOLKS!
FREEZE! don't CHEESE

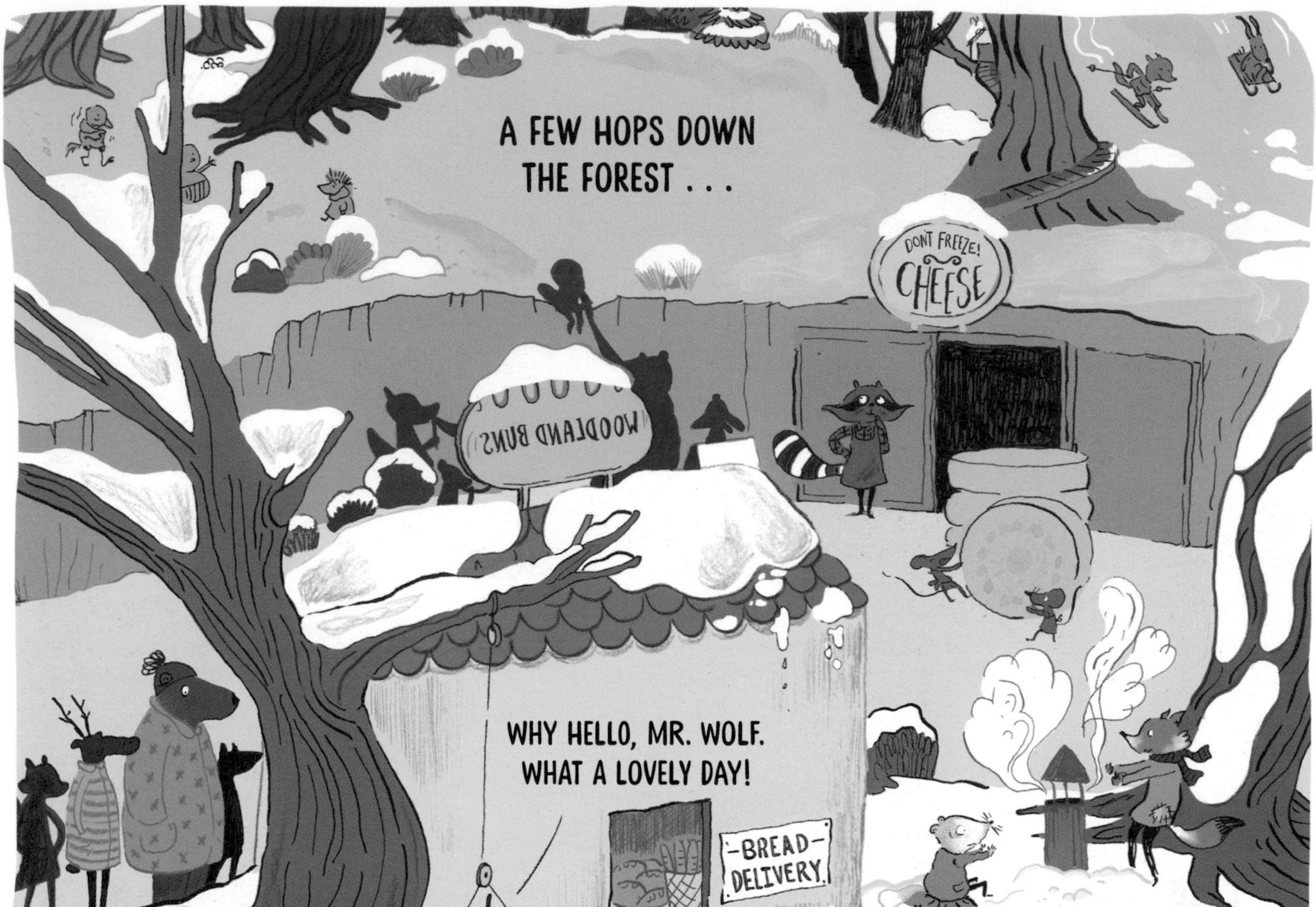
A FEW HOPS DOWN THE FOREST . . .
DON'T FREEZE! CHEESE
WOODLAND BUNS
-BREAD- DELIVERY
WHY HELLO, MR. WOLF. WHAT A LOVELY DAY!
NO, IT'S NOT.

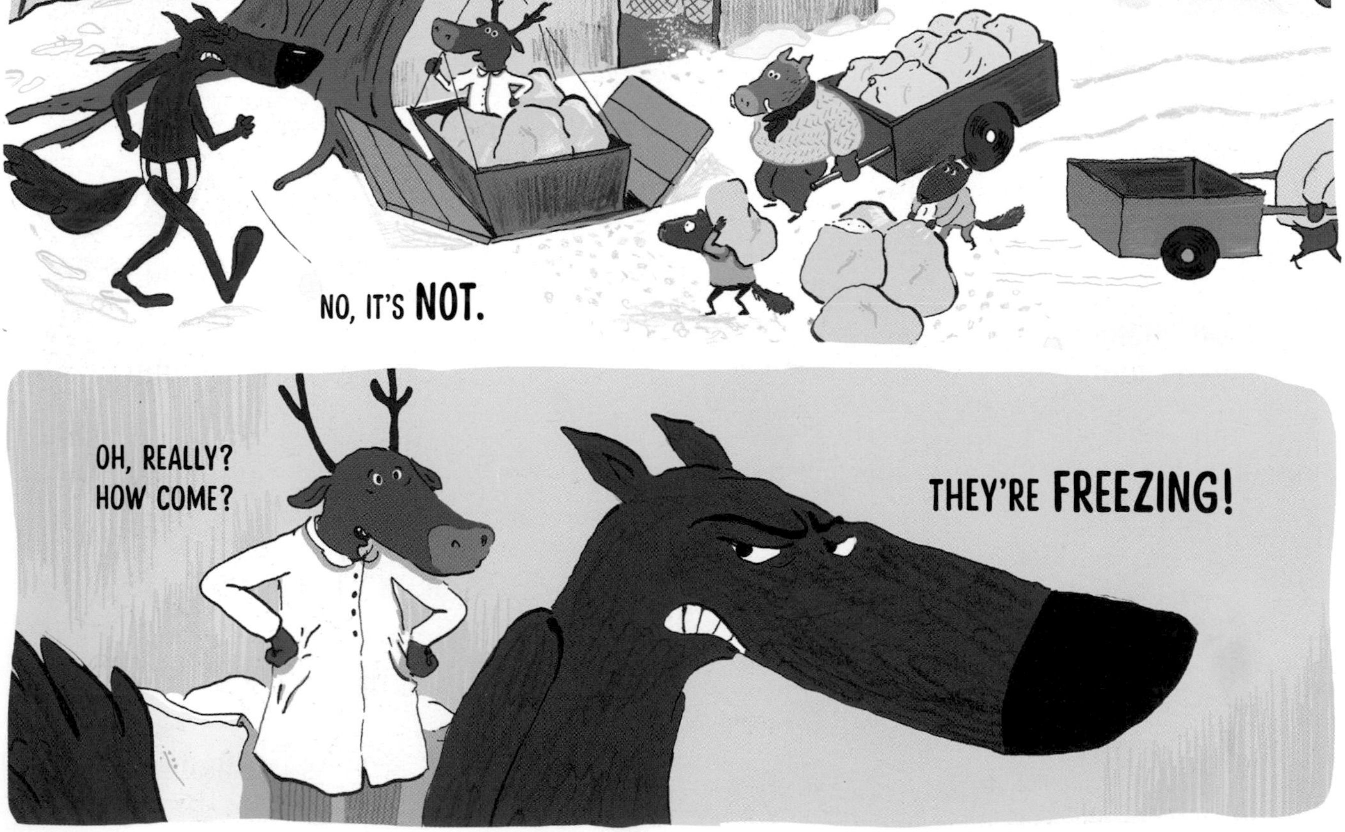
OH, REALLY? HOW COME?
THEY'RE FREEZING!

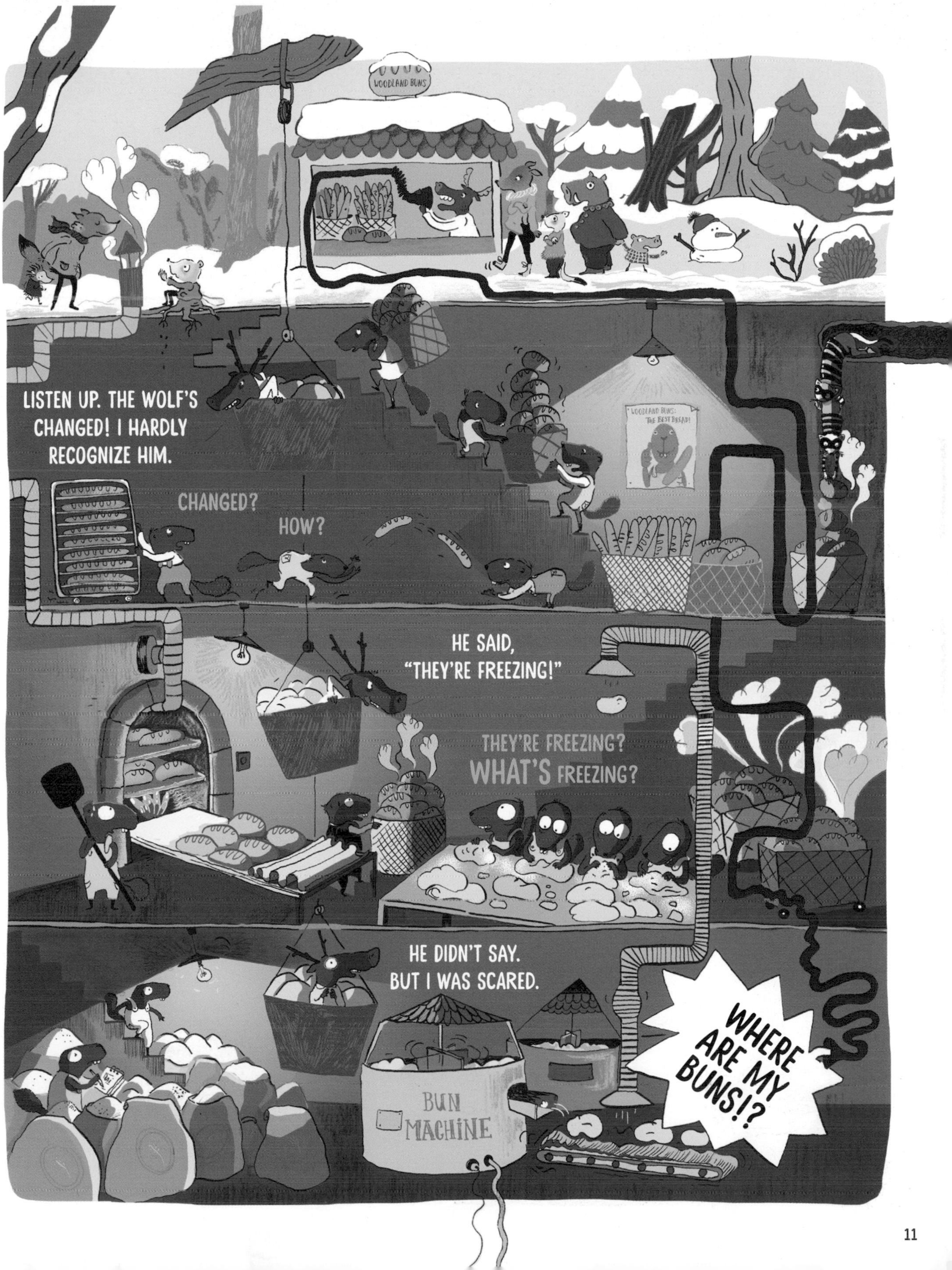
WOODLAND BUNS
WOODLAND BUNS: THE BEST BREAD!
LISTEN UP. THE WOLF'S CHANGED! I HARDLY RECOGNIZE HIM.
CHANGED?
HOW?
HE SAID, "THEY'RE FREEZING!"
THEY'RE FREEZING? WHAT'S FREEZING?
HE DIDN'T SAY. BUT I WAS SCARED.
WHERE ARE MY BUNS!?
BUN MACHINE

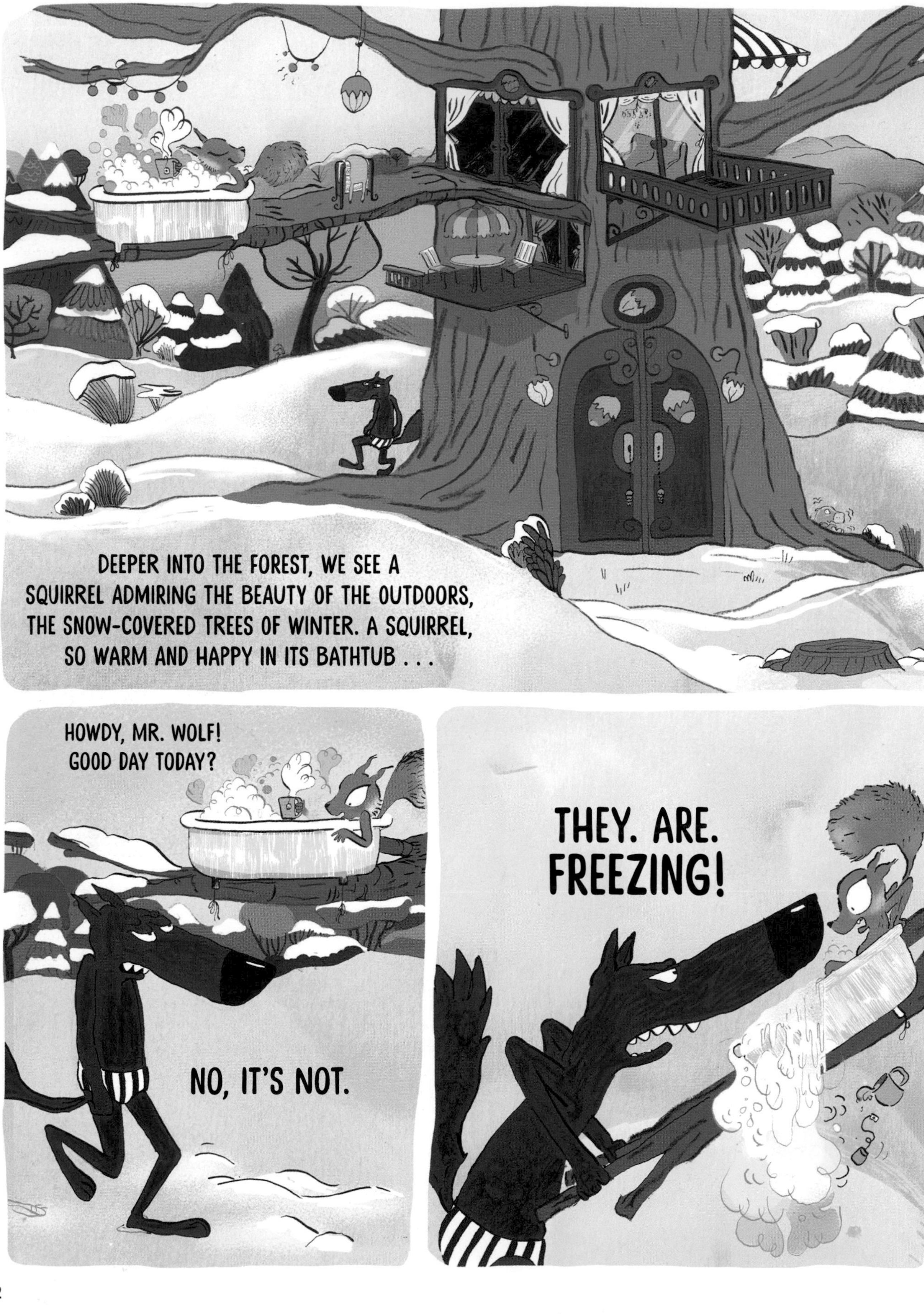
DEEPER INTO THE FOREST, WE SEE A SQUIRREL ADMIRING THE BEAUTY OF THE OUTDOORS, THE SNOW-COVERED TREES OF WINTER. A SQUIRREL, SO WARM AND HAPPY IN ITS BATHTUB . . .
HOWDY, MR. WOLF! GOOD DAY TODAY?
NO, IT'S NOT.
THEY. ARE. FREEZING!

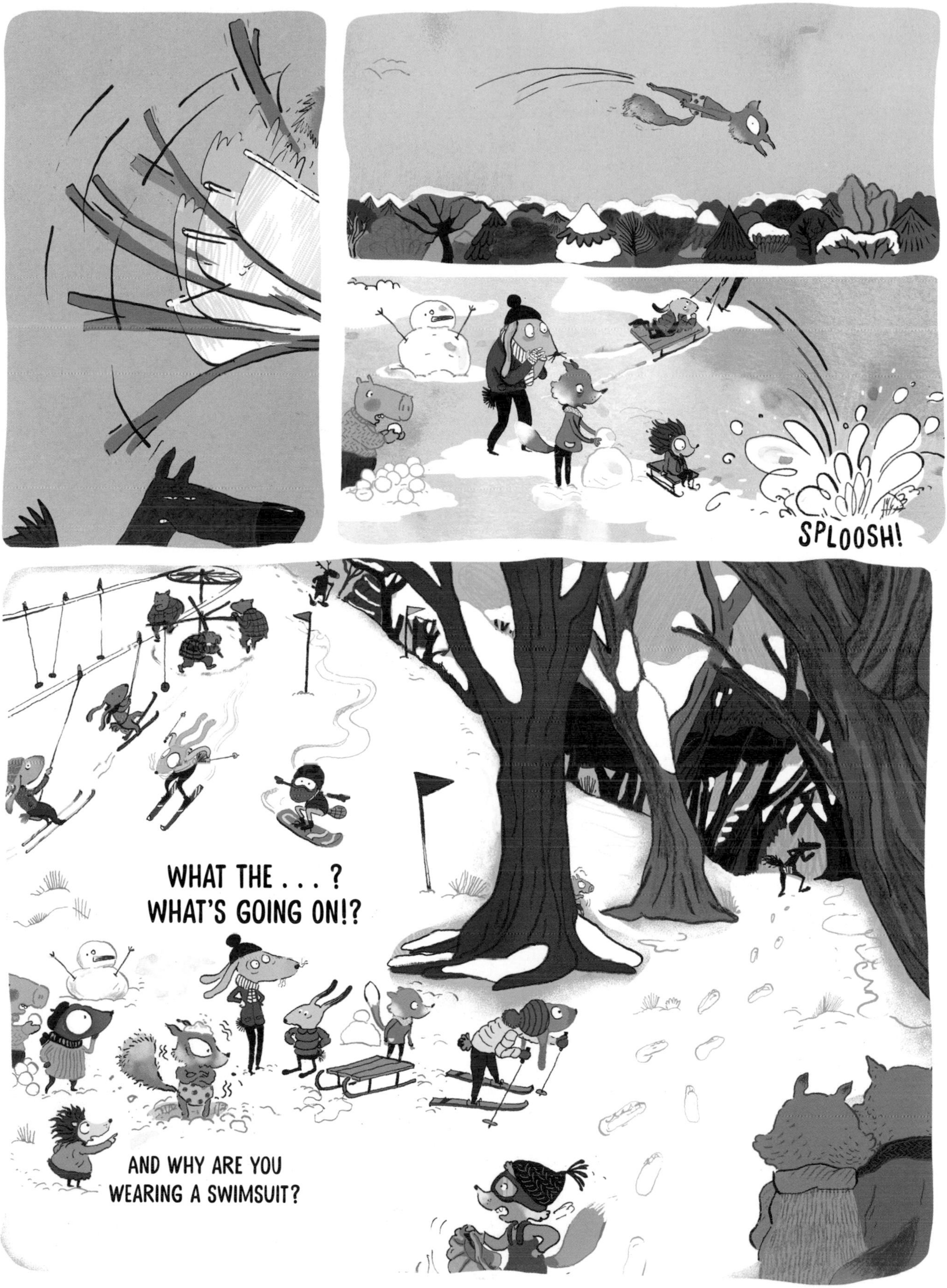
SPLOOSH!
WHAT THE . . . ?
WHAT'S GOING ON!?
AND WHY ARE YOU
WEARING A SWIMSUIT?

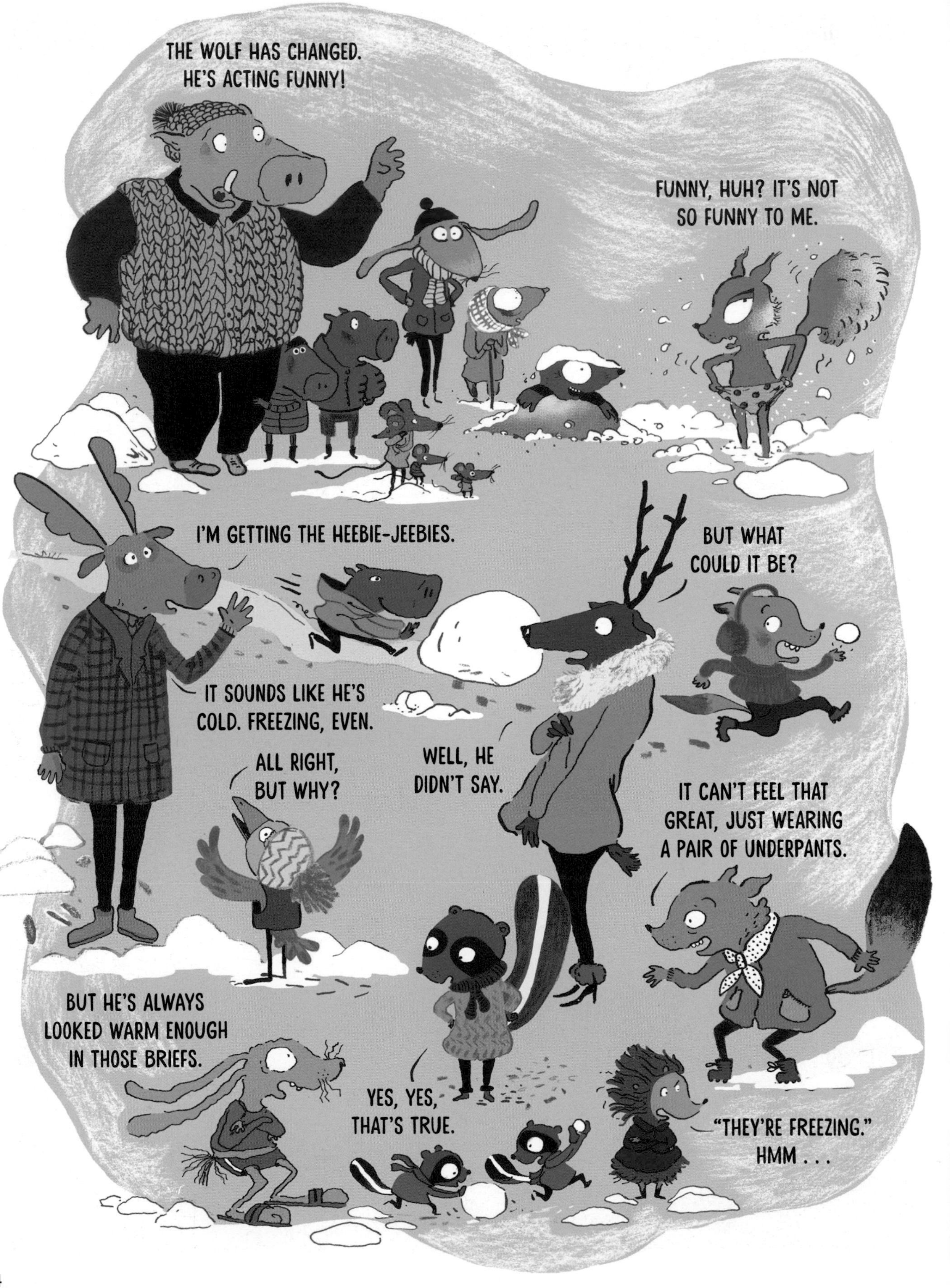
THE WOLF HAS CHANGED.
HE'S ACTING FUNNY!
FUNNY, HUH? IT'S NOT SO FUNNY TO ME.
I'M GETTING THE HEEBIE-JEEBIES.
BUT WHAT COULD IT BE?
IT SOUNDS LIKE HE'S COLD. FREEZING, EVEN.
ALL RIGHT, BUT WHY?
WELL, HE DIDN'T SAY.
IT CAN'T FEEL THAT GREAT, JUST WEARING A PAIR OF UNDERPANTS.
BUT HE'S ALWAYS LOOKED WARM ENOUGH IN THOSE BRIEFS.
YES, YES, THAT'S TRUE.
"THEY'RE FREEZING." HMM . . .

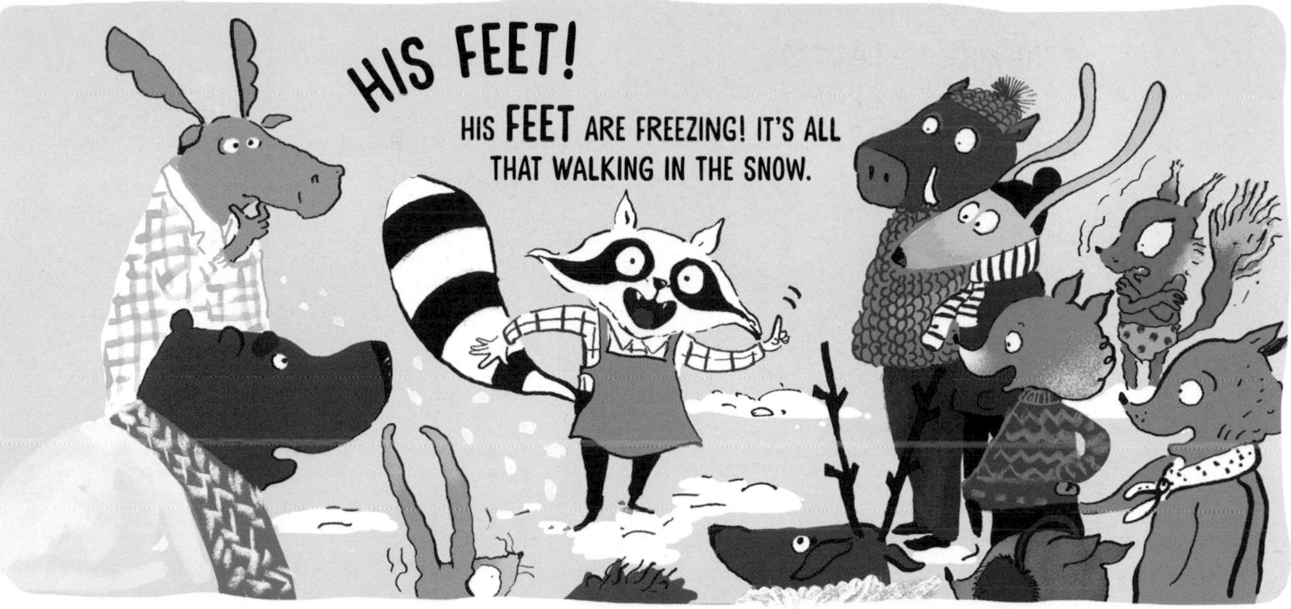
HIS FEET!
HIS FEET ARE FREEZING! IT'S ALL THAT WALKING IN THE SNOW.

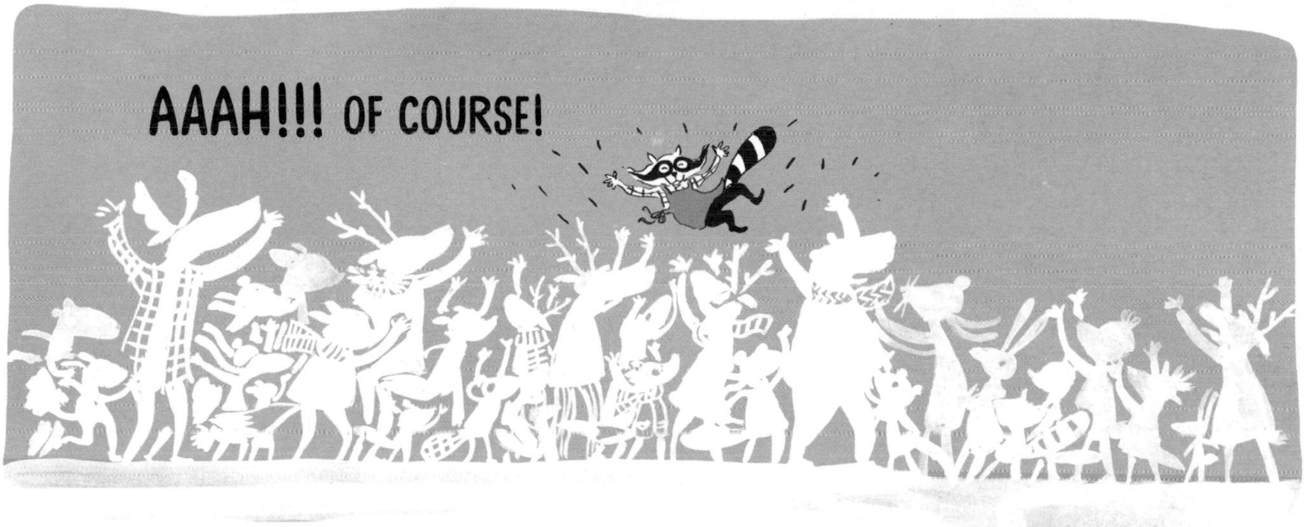
AAAH!!! OF COURSE!

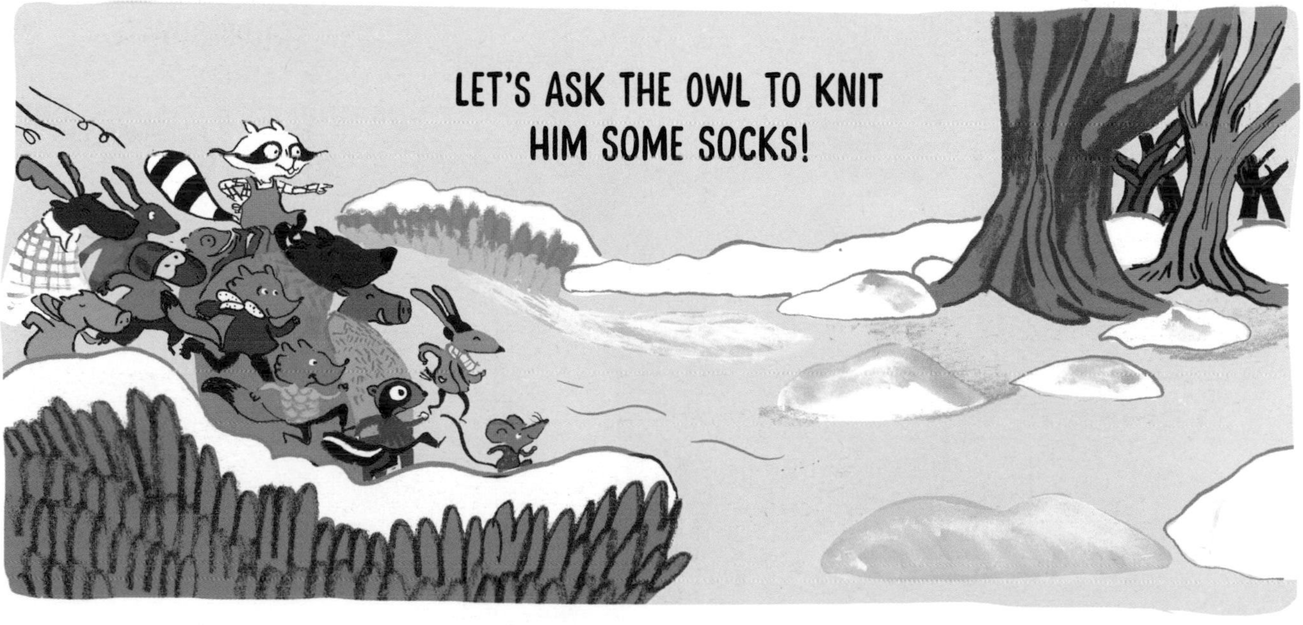
LET'S ASK THE OWL TO KNIT HIM SOME SOCKS!

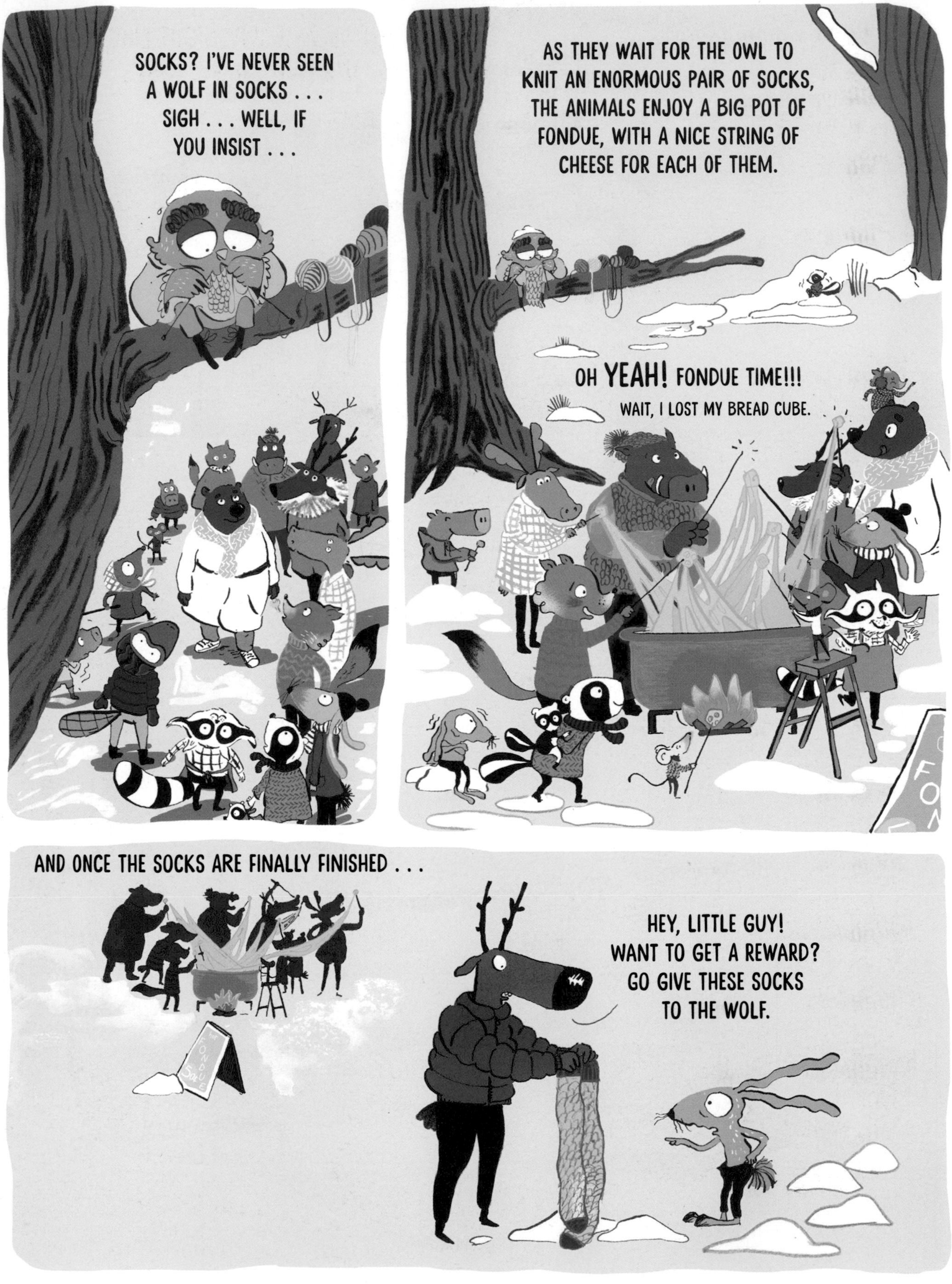
SOCKS? I'VE NEVER SEEN A WOLF IN SOCKS . . . SIGH . . . WELL, IF YOU INSIST . . .
AS THEY WAIT FOR THE OWL TO KNIT AN ENORMOUS PAIR OF SOCKS, THE ANIMALS ENJOY A BIG POT OF FONDUE, WITH A NICE STRING OF CHEESE FOR EACH OF THEM.
OH **YEAH!** FONDUE TIME!!!
WAIT, I LOST MY BREAD CUBE.
AND ONCE THE SOCKS ARE FINALLY FINISHED . . .
FONDUE
HEY, LITTLE GUY! WANT TO GET A REWARD? GO GIVE THESE SOCKS TO THE WOLF.

BUT ON A SNOWY NIGHT LIKE THIS, IT'S EASY TO GET LOST . . .
BRRR, I'M COLD. WHAT'S WITH THIS WINTER . . . AND WHERE IS THE WOLF?
NOTHING BUT SNOW ALL AROUND . . . AND IT'S ABOUT TO GET DARK . . .
HOPEFULLY I'LL FIND HIM TOMORROW . . . IT'S SO, SO COLD . . .

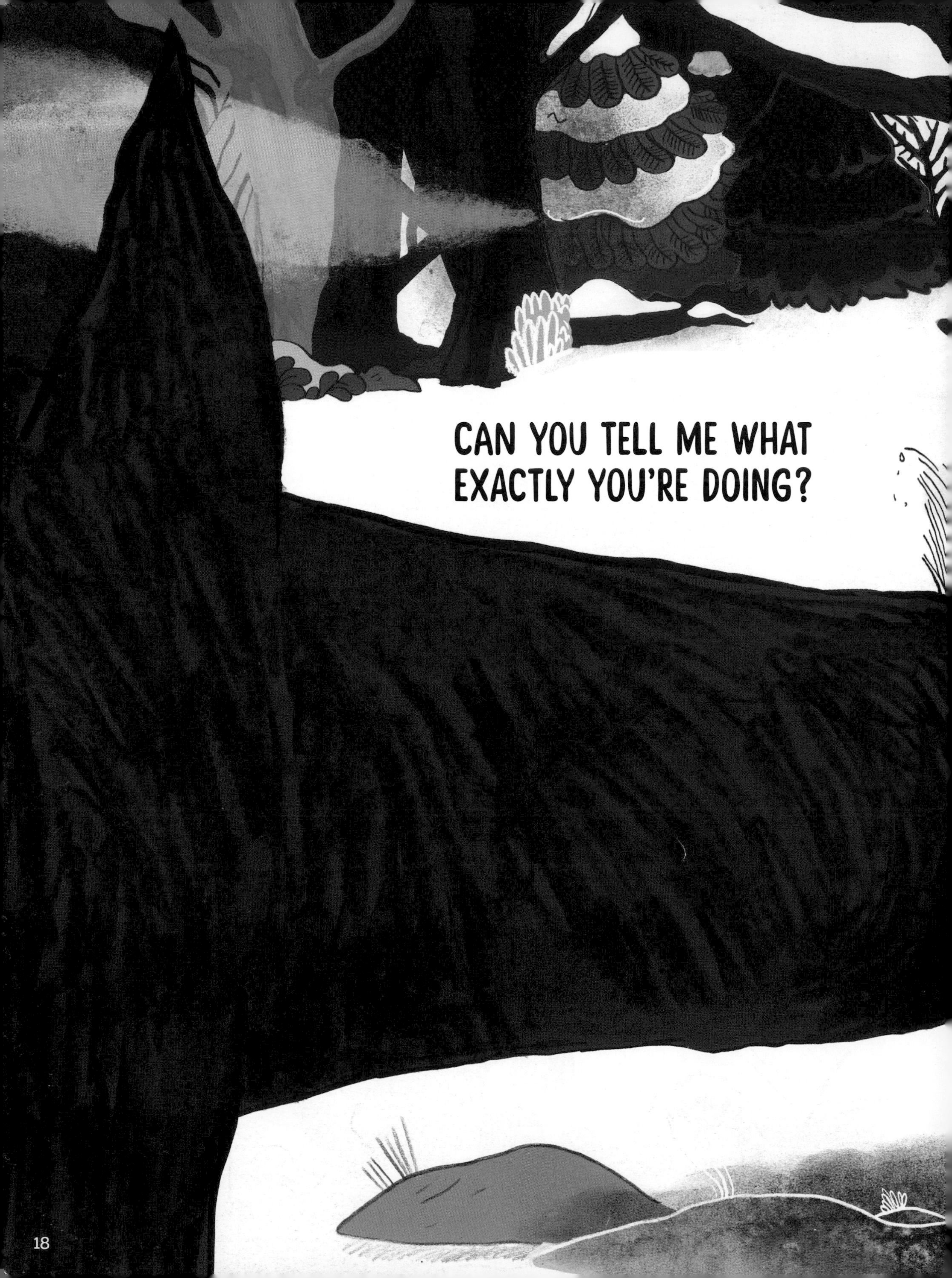
CAN YOU TELL ME WHAT
EXACTLY YOU'RE DOING?

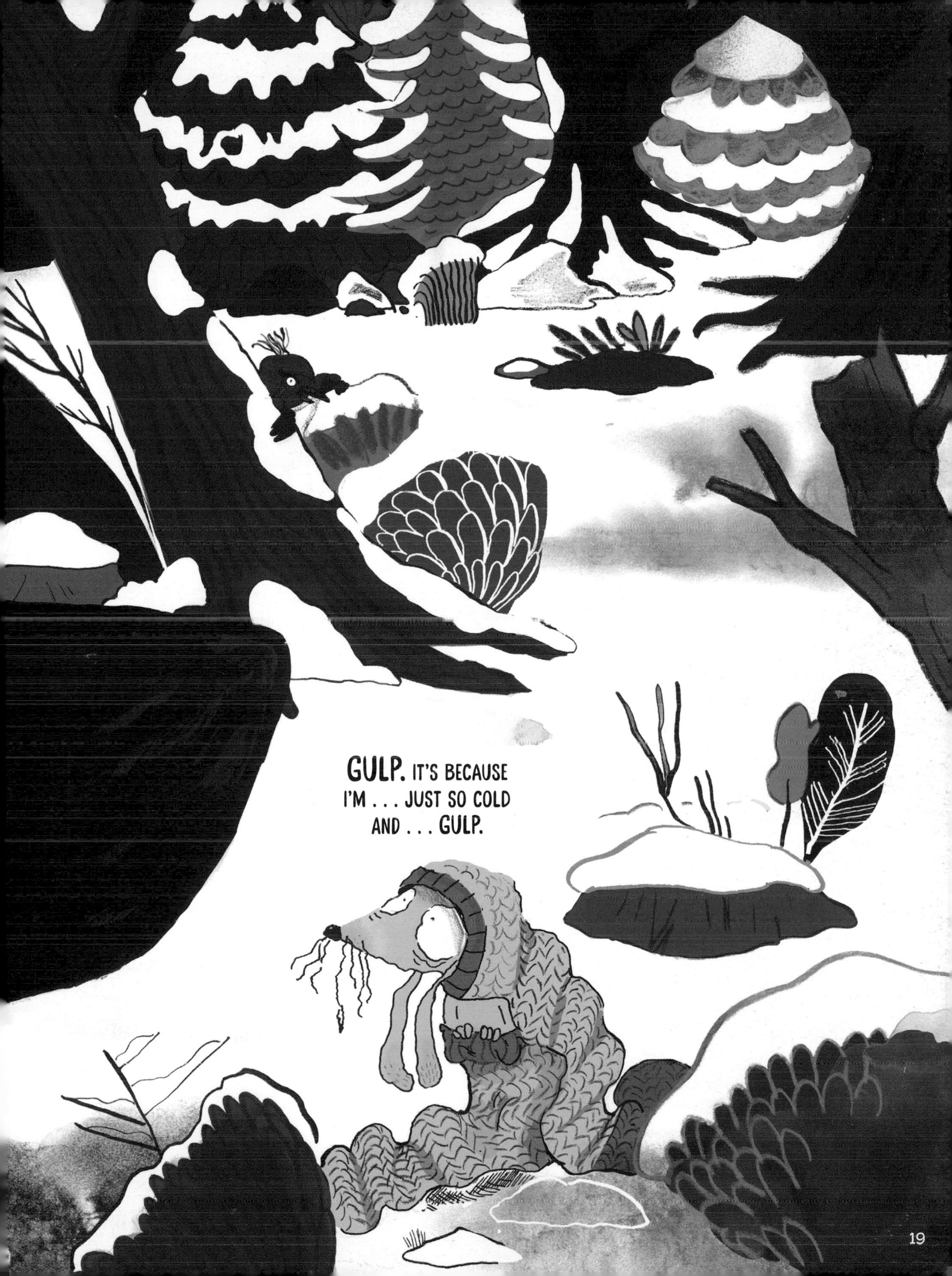
GULP. IT'S BECAUSE I'M . . . JUST SO COLD AND . . . GULP.

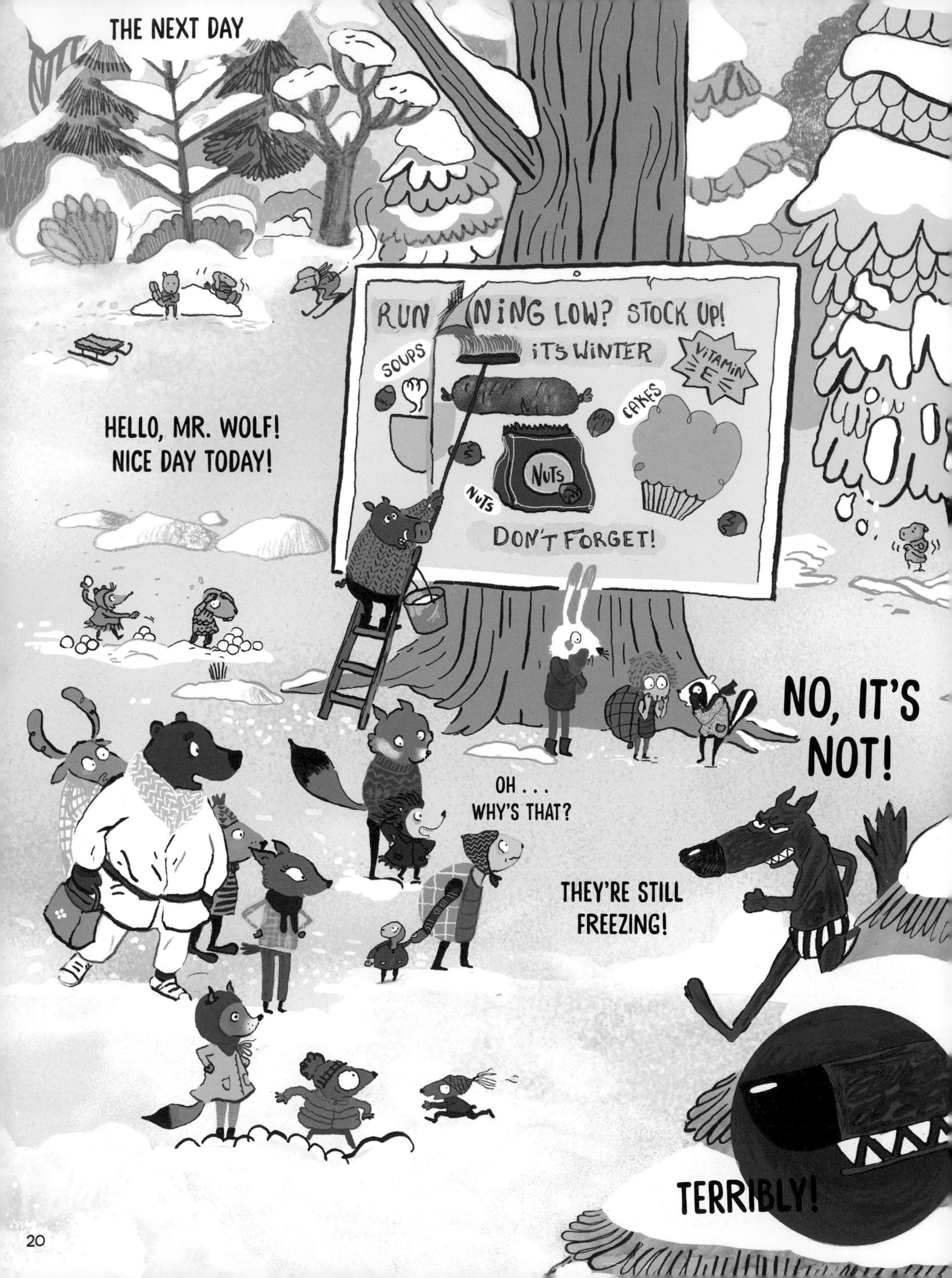
THE NEXT DAY
RUN NiNG LOW? STOCK UP!
iT'S WiNTER
SOUPS
ViTAMiN E
CAKES
NUTS
NUTS
DON'T FORGET!
HELLO, MR. WOLF!
NICE DAY TODAY!
NO, IT'S
NOT!
OH . . .
WHY'S THAT?
THEY'RE STILL
FREEZING!
TERRIBLY!

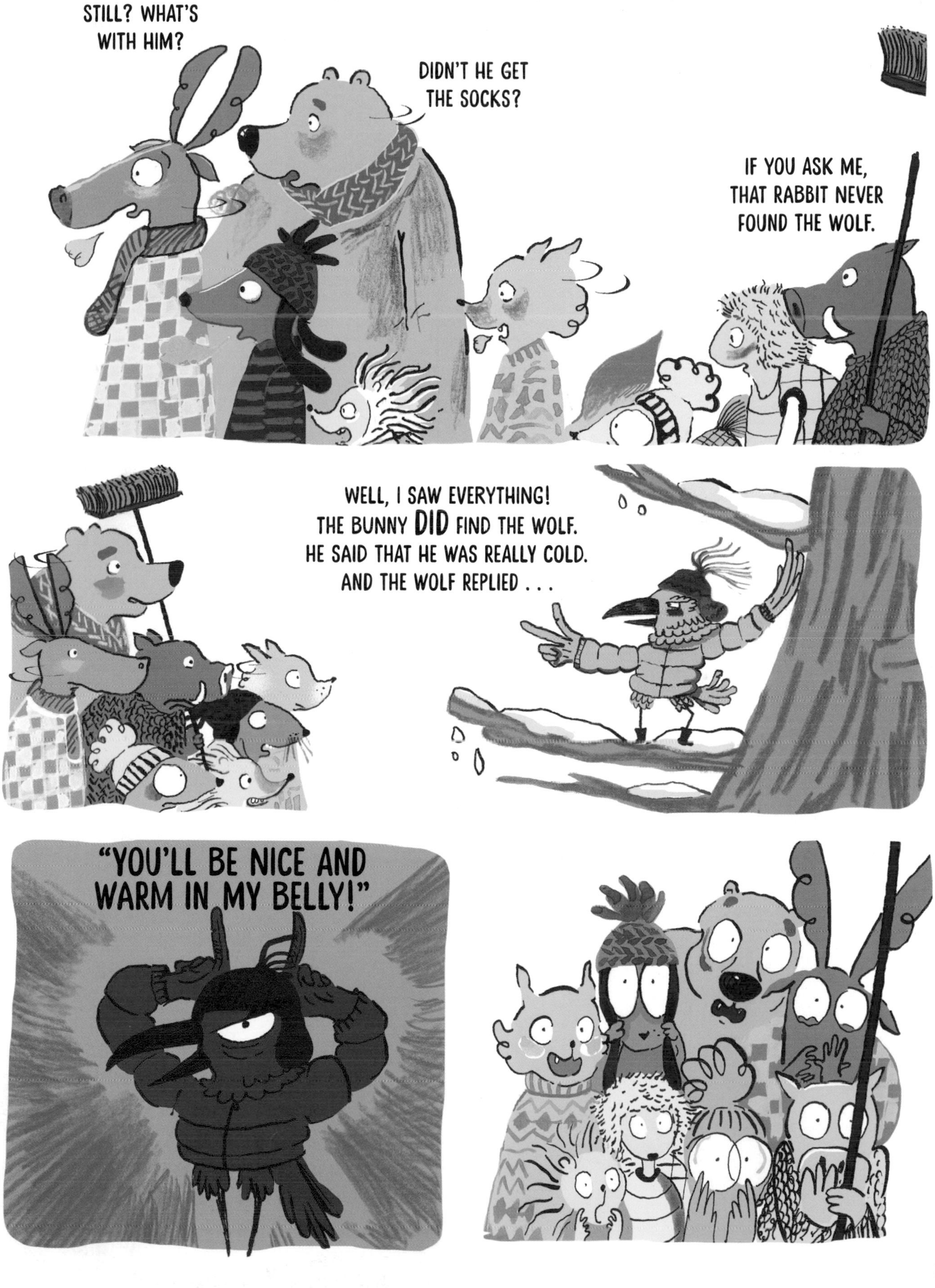
STILL? WHAT'S WITH HIM?
DIDN'T HE GET THE SOCKS?
IF YOU ASK ME, THAT RABBIT NEVER FOUND THE WOLF.
WELL, I SAW EVERYTHING! THE BUNNY DID FIND THE WOLF. HE SAID THAT HE WAS REALLY COLD. AND THE WOLF REPLIED . . .
"YOU'LL BE NICE AND WARM IN MY BELLY!"

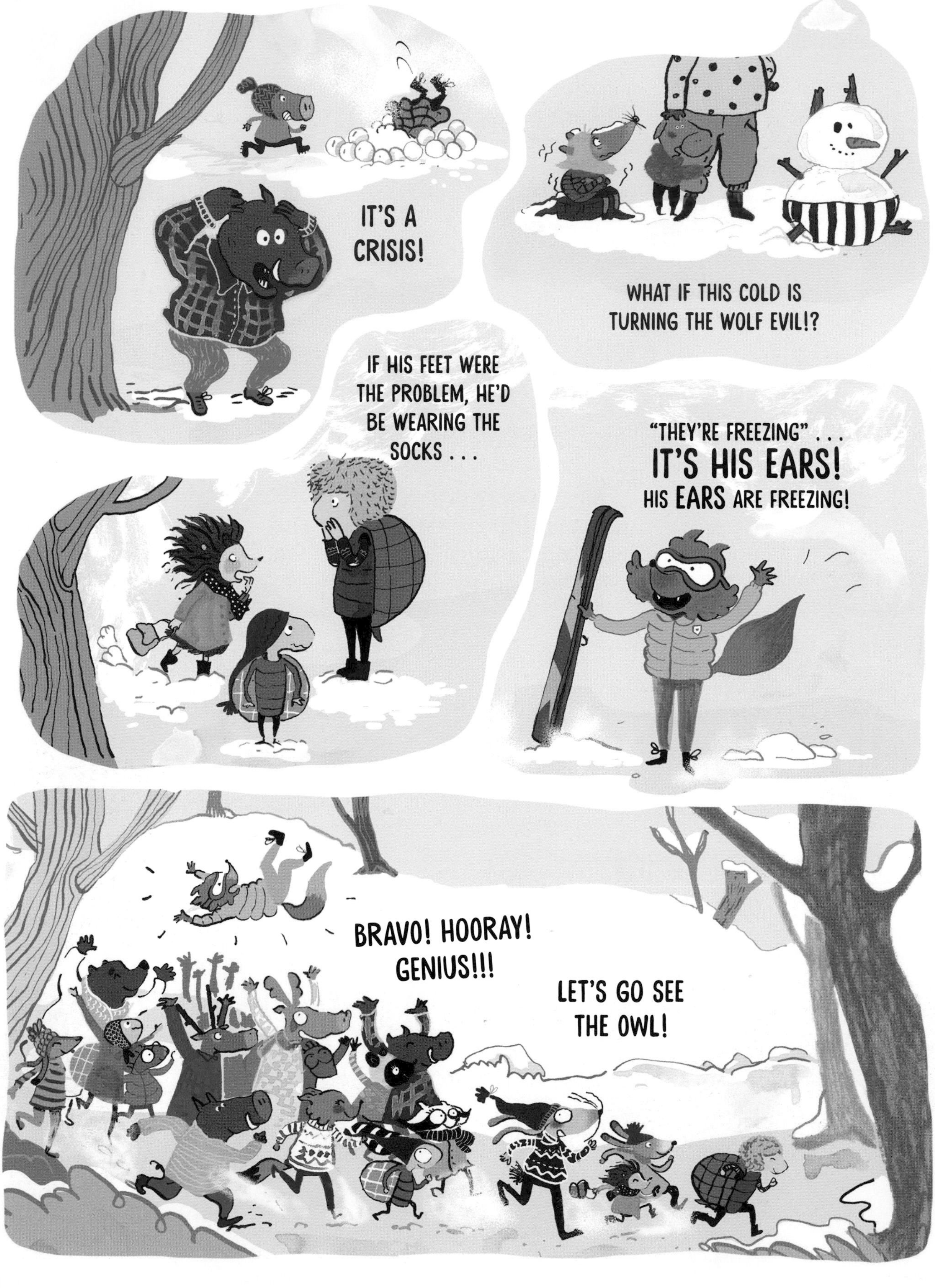

IT'S A CRISIS!
WHAT IF THIS COLD IS TURNING THE WOLF EVIL!?
IF HIS FEET WERE THE PROBLEM, HE'D BE WEARING THE SOCKS . . .
"THEY'RE FREEZING" . . .
IT'S HIS EARS!
HIS EARS ARE FREEZING!
BRAVO! HOORAY! GENIUS!!!
LET'S GO SEE THE OWL!

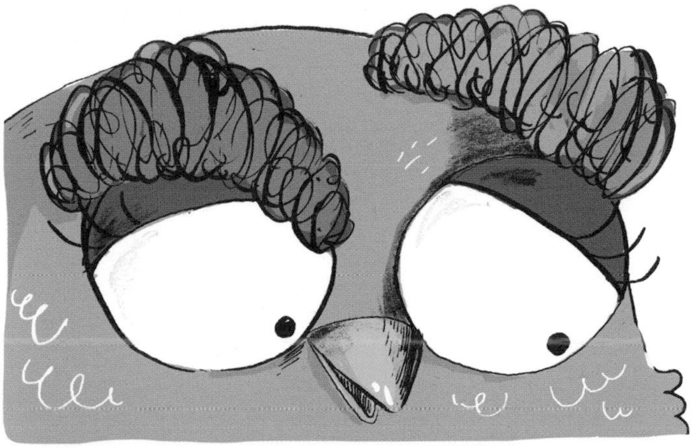
A HAT?
I'VE NEVER SEEN A WOLF IN A HAT. BUT HEY, IF IT HELPS YOU RELAX . . .

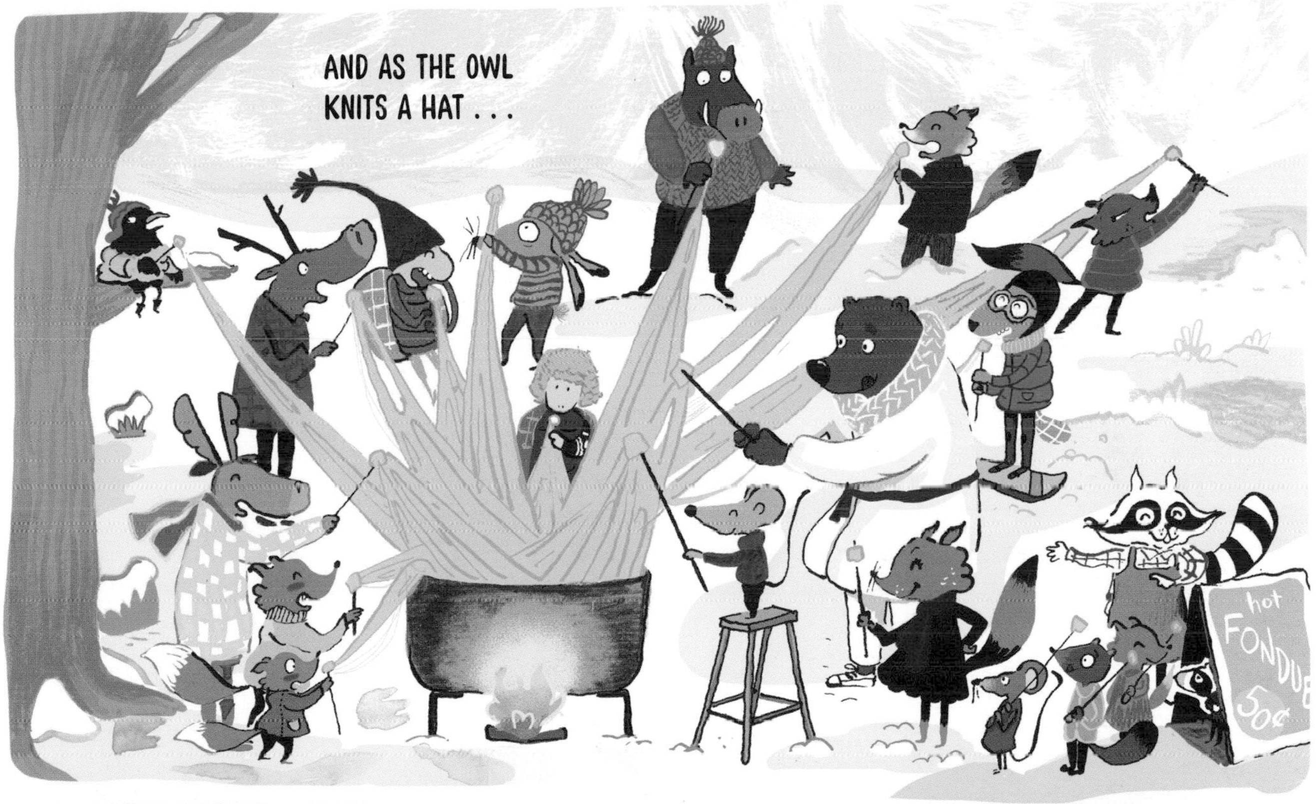
AND AS THE OWL KNITS A HAT . . .
hot FONDUE 50¢

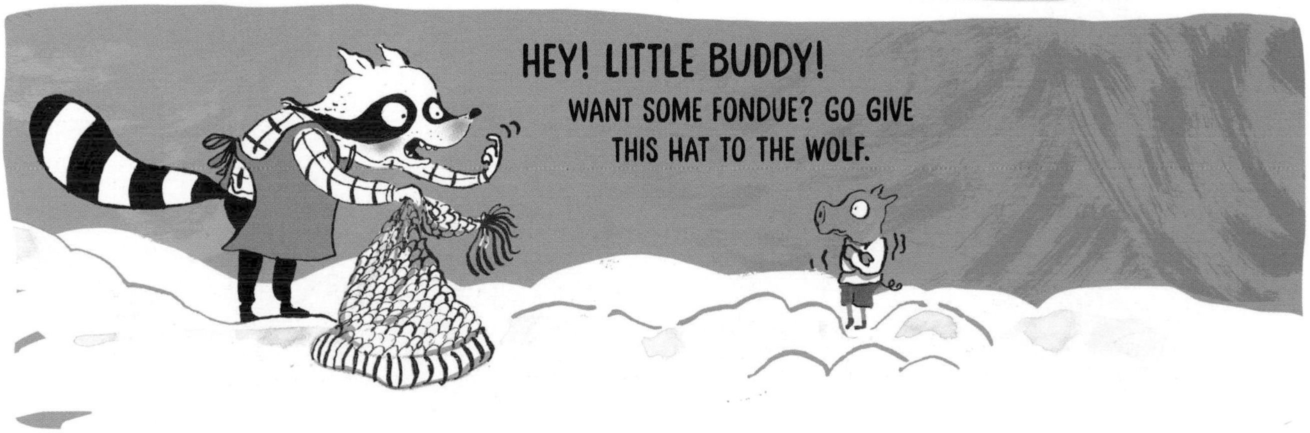
HEY! LITTLE BUDDY!
WANT SOME FONDUE? GO GIVE THIS HAT TO THE WOLF.

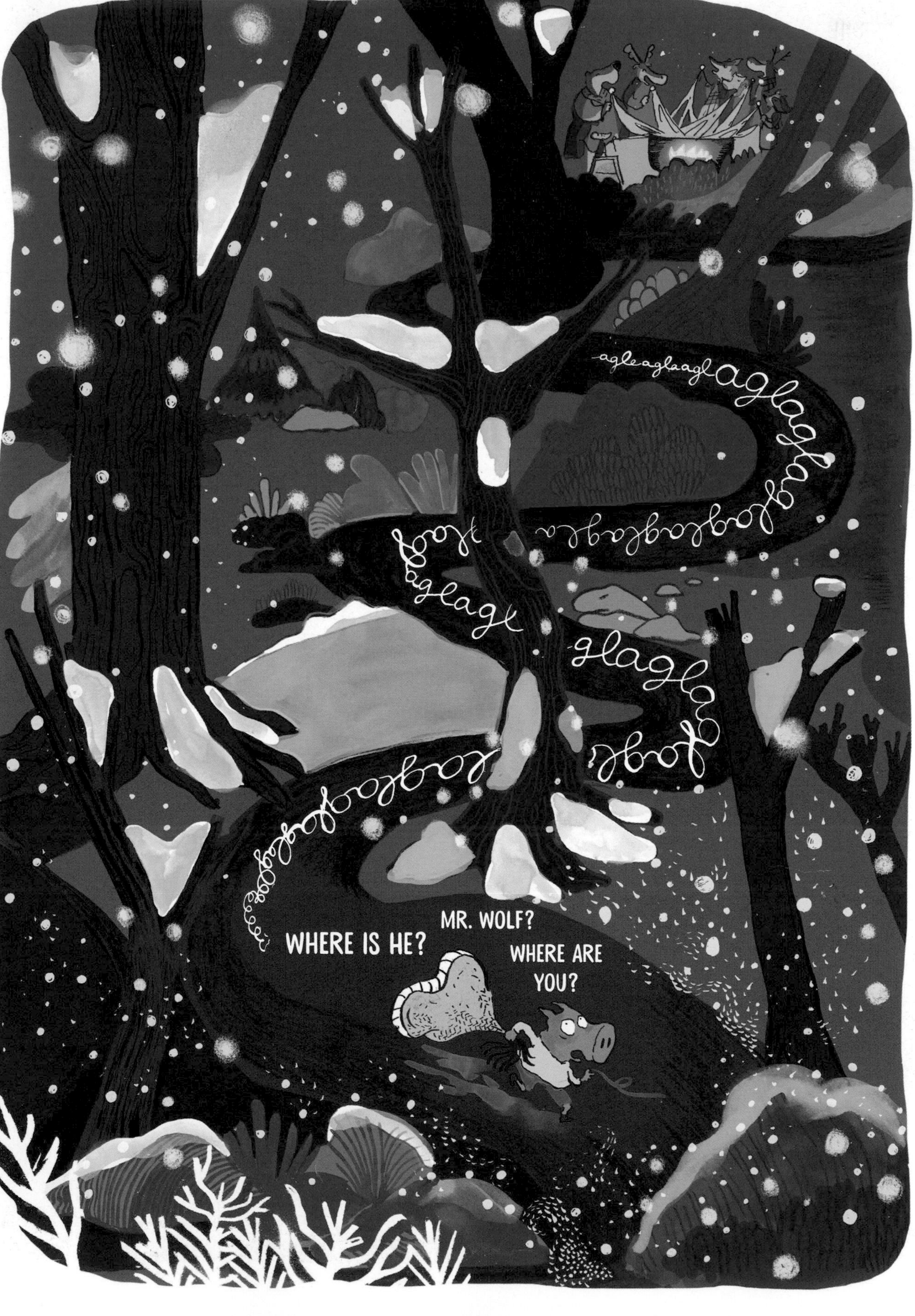
WHERE IS HE?
MR. WOLF?
WHERE ARE YOU?

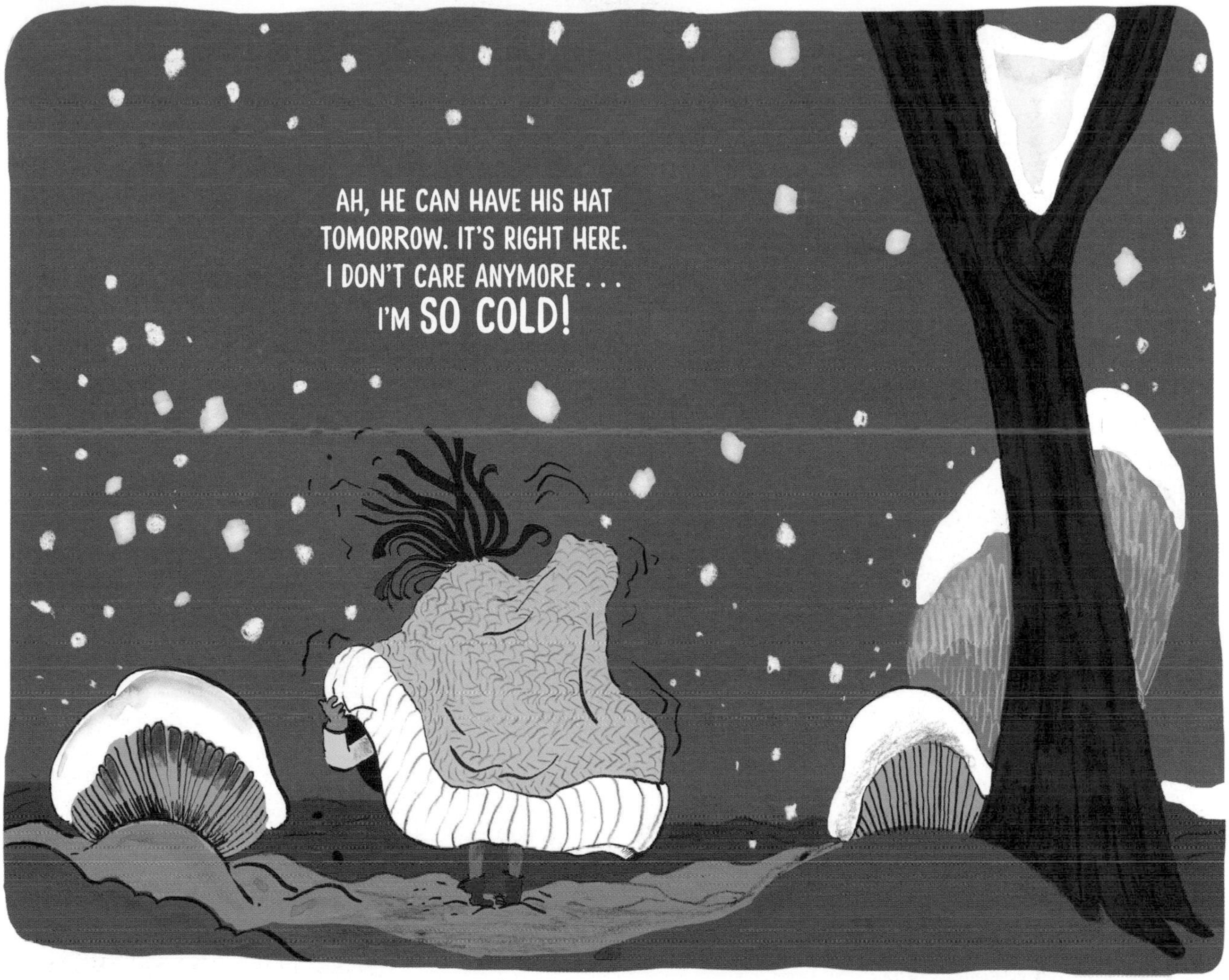
AH, HE CAN HAVE HIS HAT
TOMORROW. IT'S RIGHT HERE.
I DON'T CARE ANYMORE . . .
I'M SO COLD!

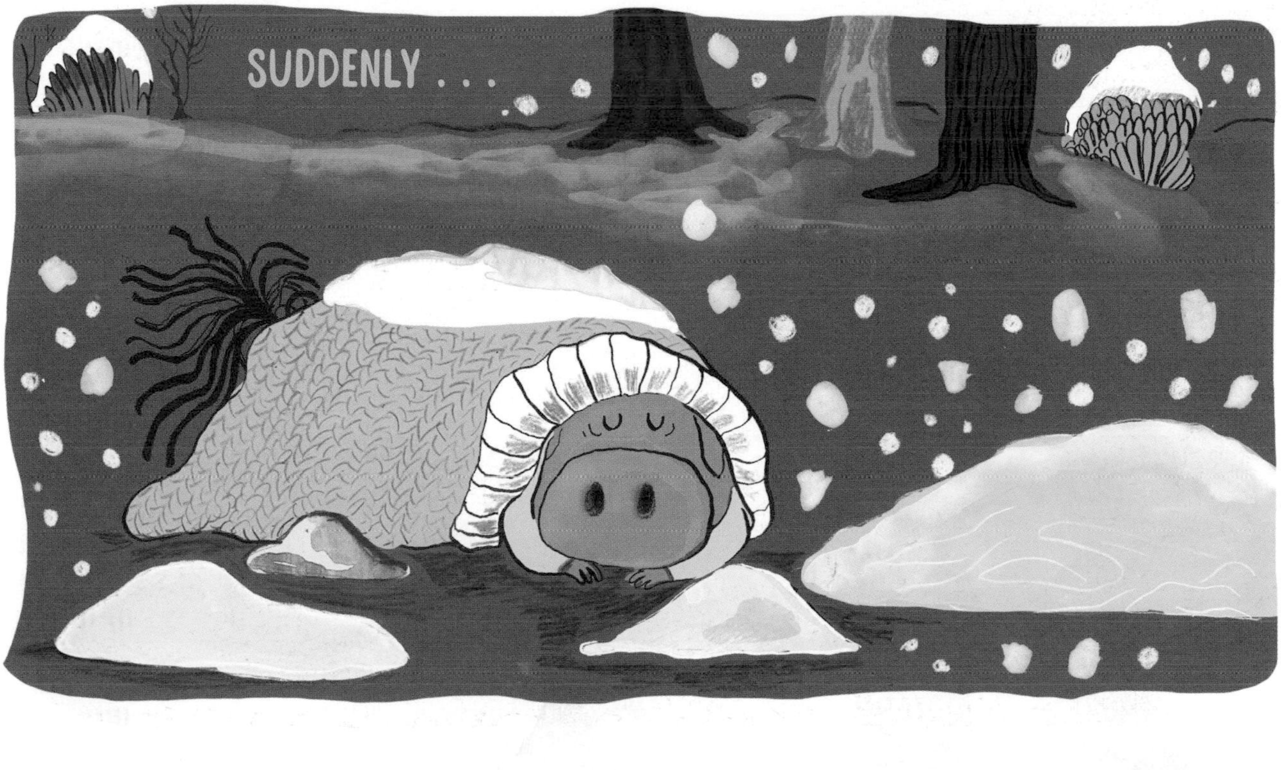
SUDDENLY . . .

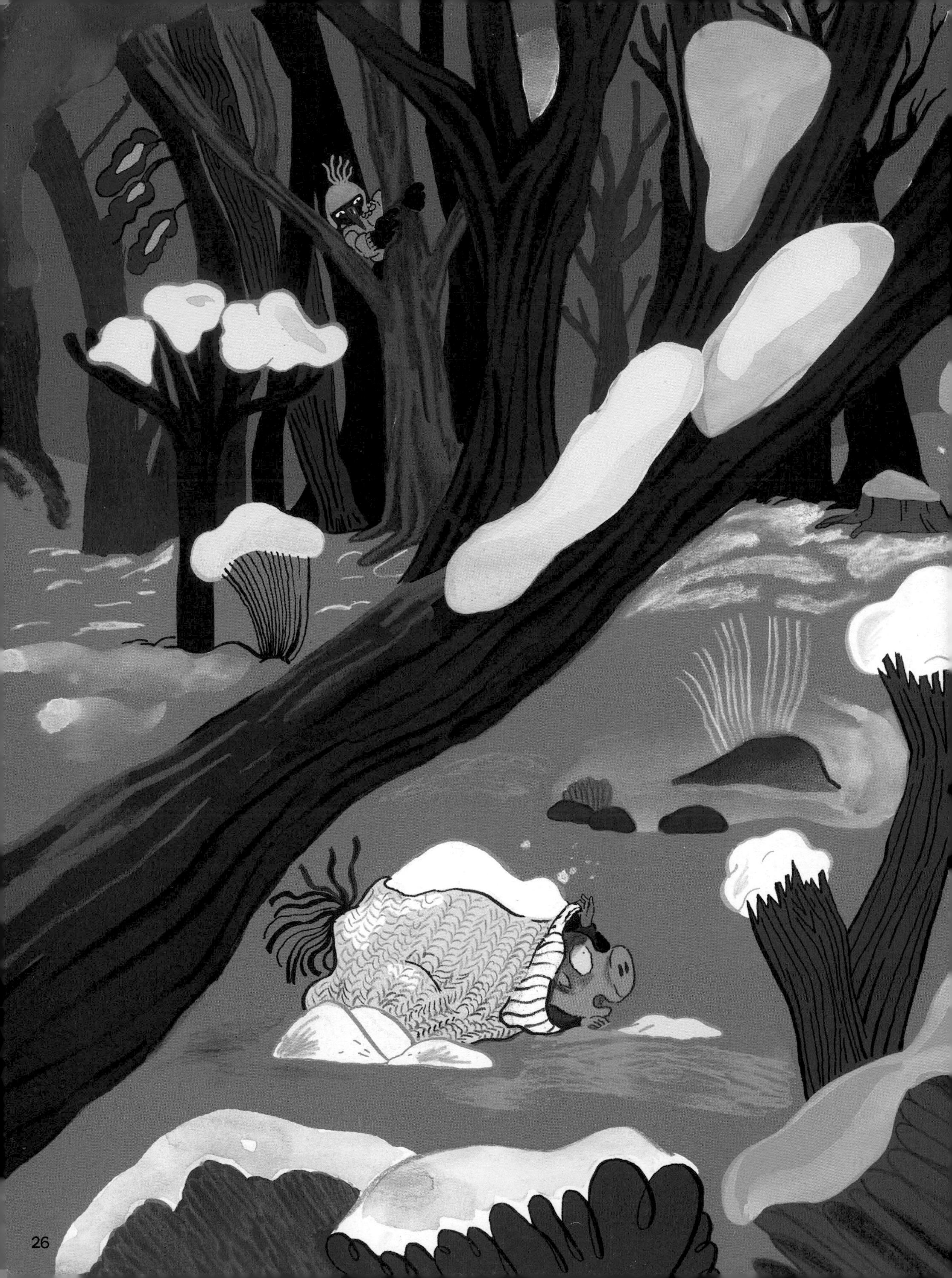

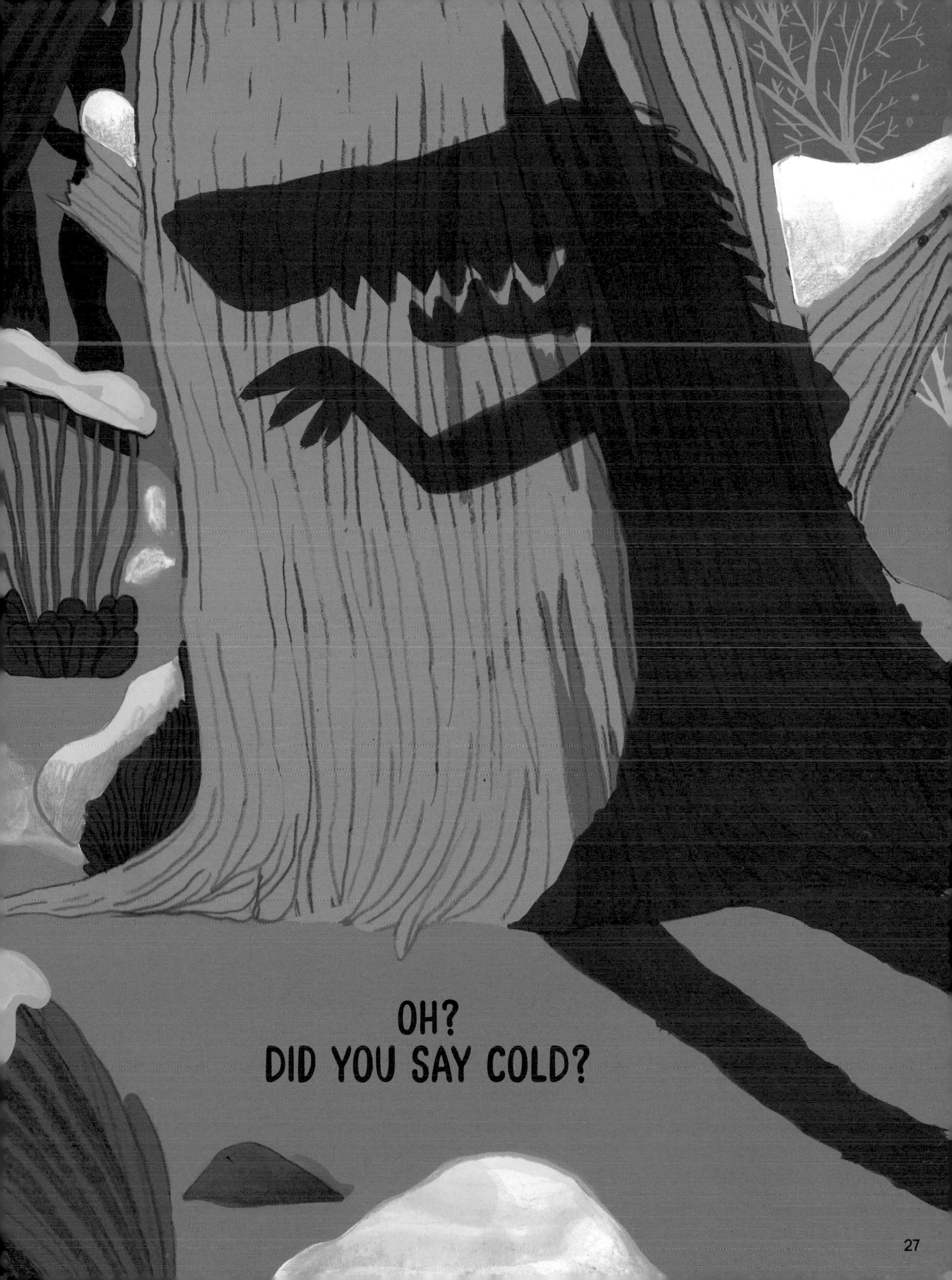

OH?
DID YOU SAY COLD?

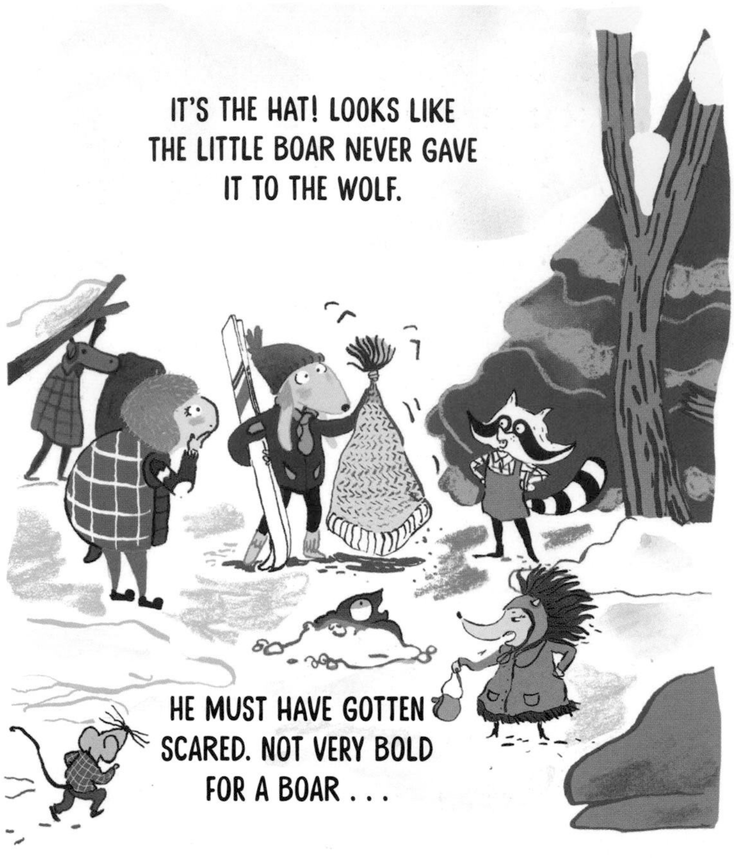
IT'S THE HAT! LOOKS LIKE THE LITTLE BOAR NEVER GAVE IT TO THE WOLF.
HE MUST HAVE GOTTEN SCARED. NOT VERY BOLD FOR A BOAR . . .

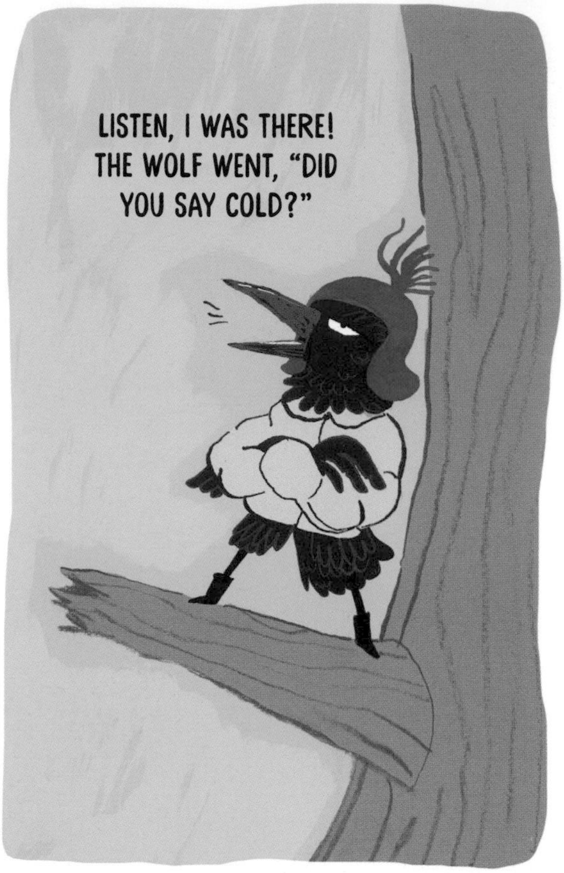
LISTEN, I WAS THERE! THE WOLF WENT, "DID YOU SAY COLD?"

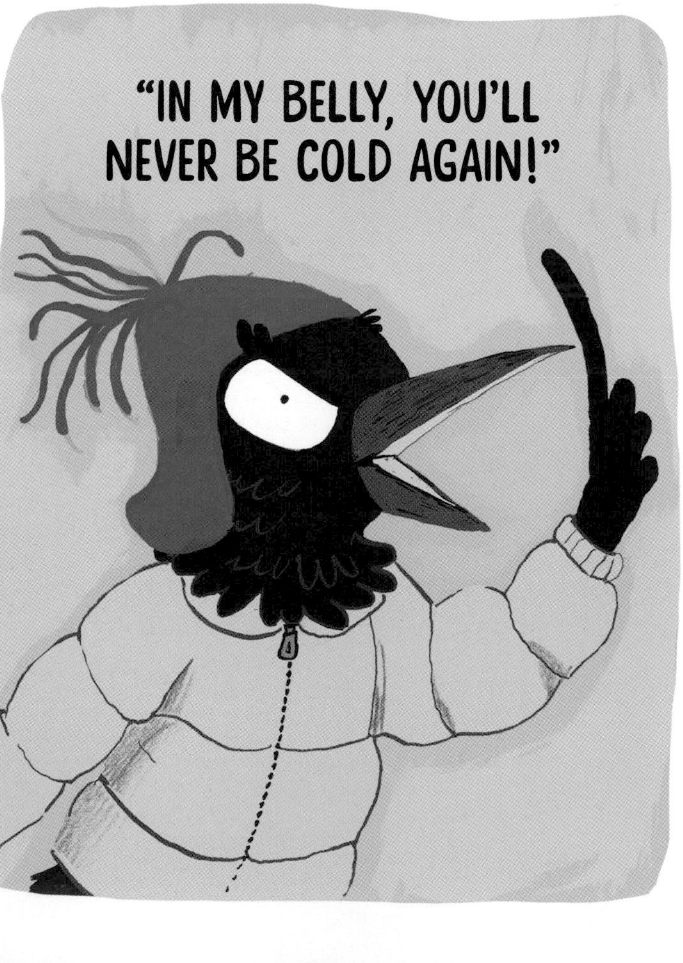
"IN MY BELLY, YOU'LL NEVER BE COLD AGAIN!"

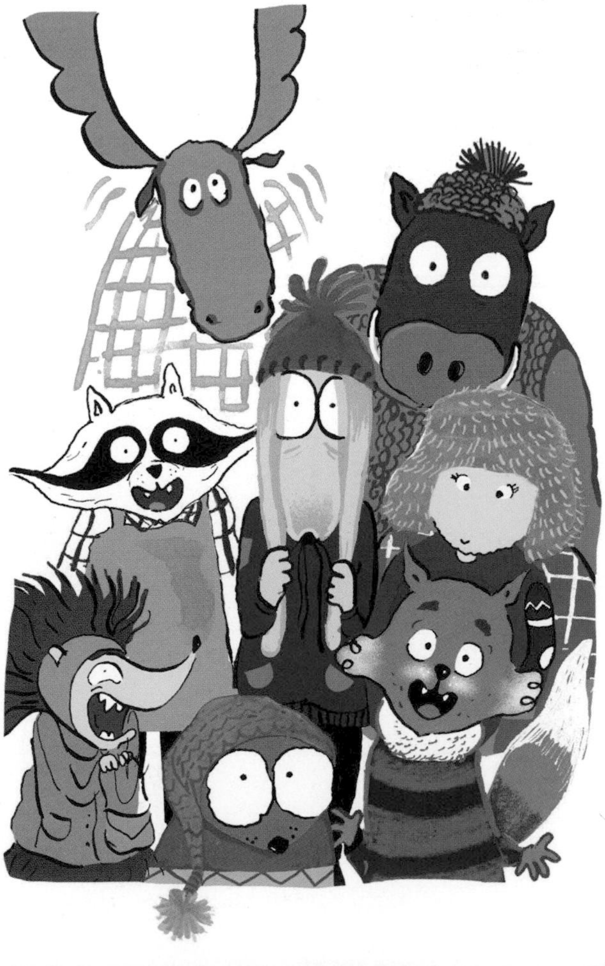

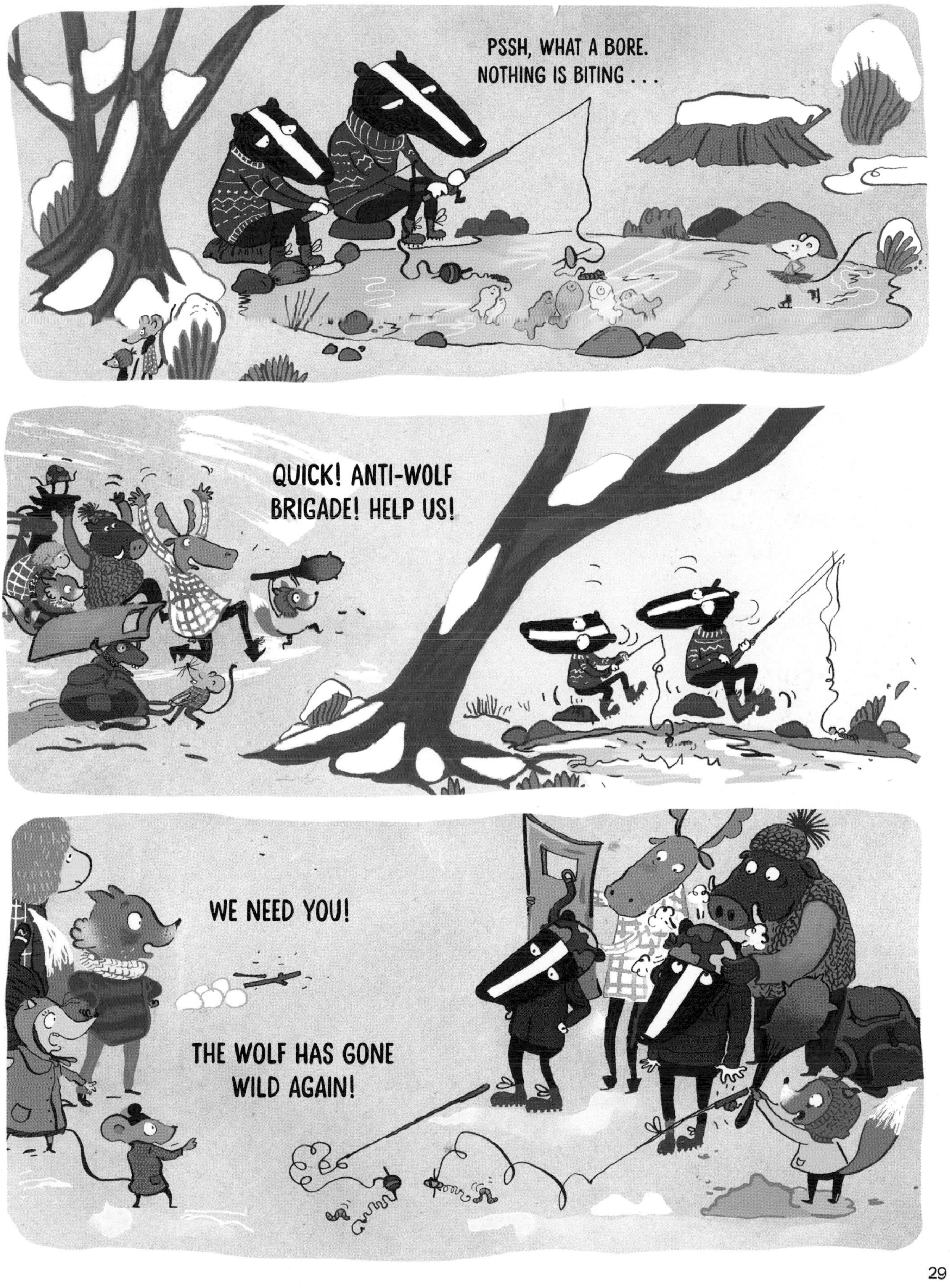
PSSH, WHAT A BORE.
NOTHING IS BITING . . .
QUICK! ANTI-WOLF BRIGADE! HELP US!
WE NEED YOU!
THE WOLF HAS GONE WILD AGAIN!

WHOOO! IT'S THE RETURN OF THE ANTI-WOLF BRIGADE!
NO NEED TO PANIC! WE'RE HERE TO PROTECT YOU!
QUICK, TO THE WOLF'S HOUSE!
WHERE DO WE START?
AND WHEN WE GET THERE, THEN WHAT?
YOU SAY, "TELL US, IN THE NAME OF THE LAW--WHAT'S FREEZING?"
THAT'S ALL WE NEED TO KNOW!

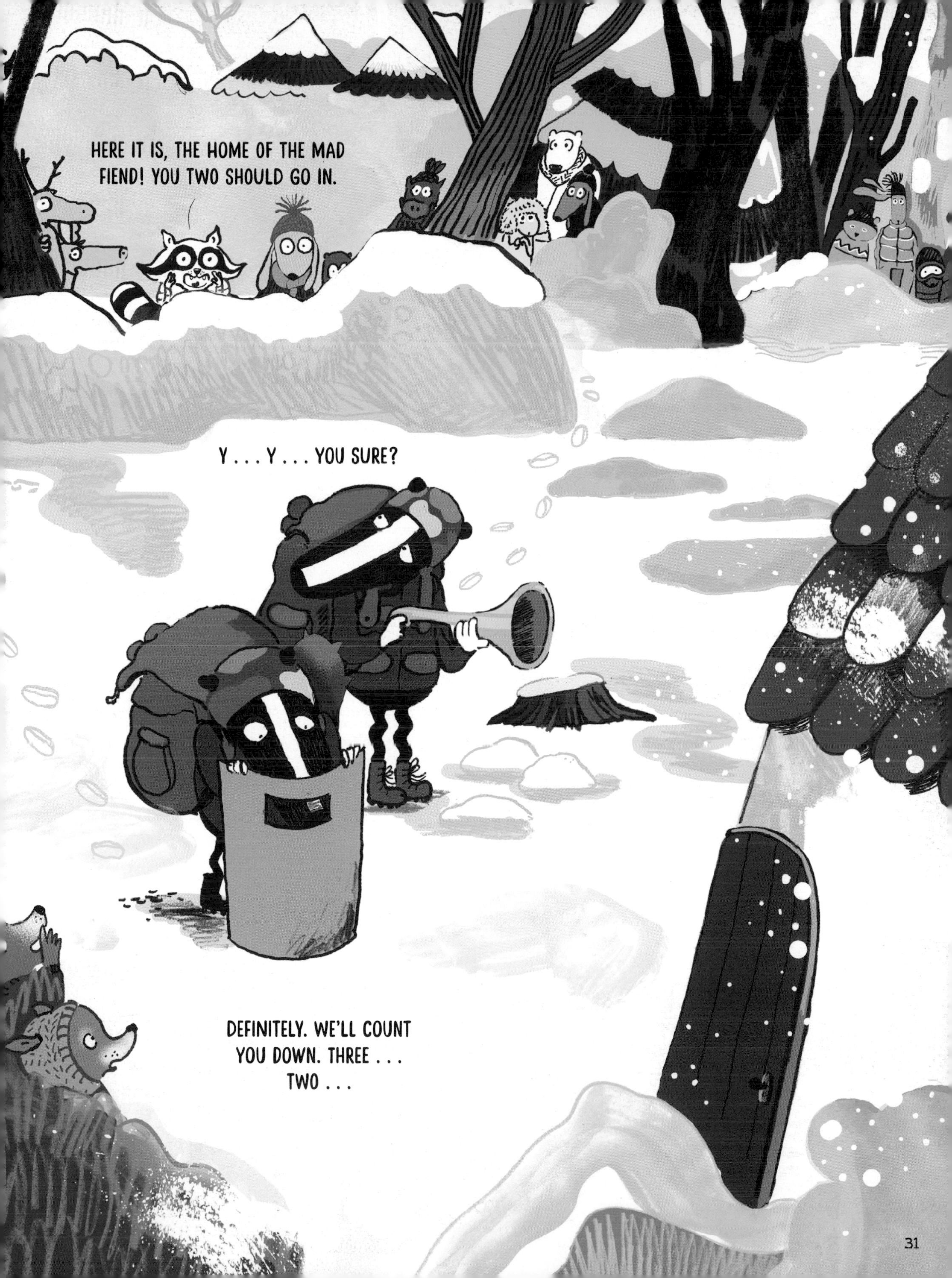
HERE IT IS, THE HOME OF THE MAD FIEND! YOU TWO SHOULD GO IN.
Y . . . Y . . . YOU SURE?
DEFINITELY. WE'LL COUNT YOU DOWN. THREE . . . TWO . . .

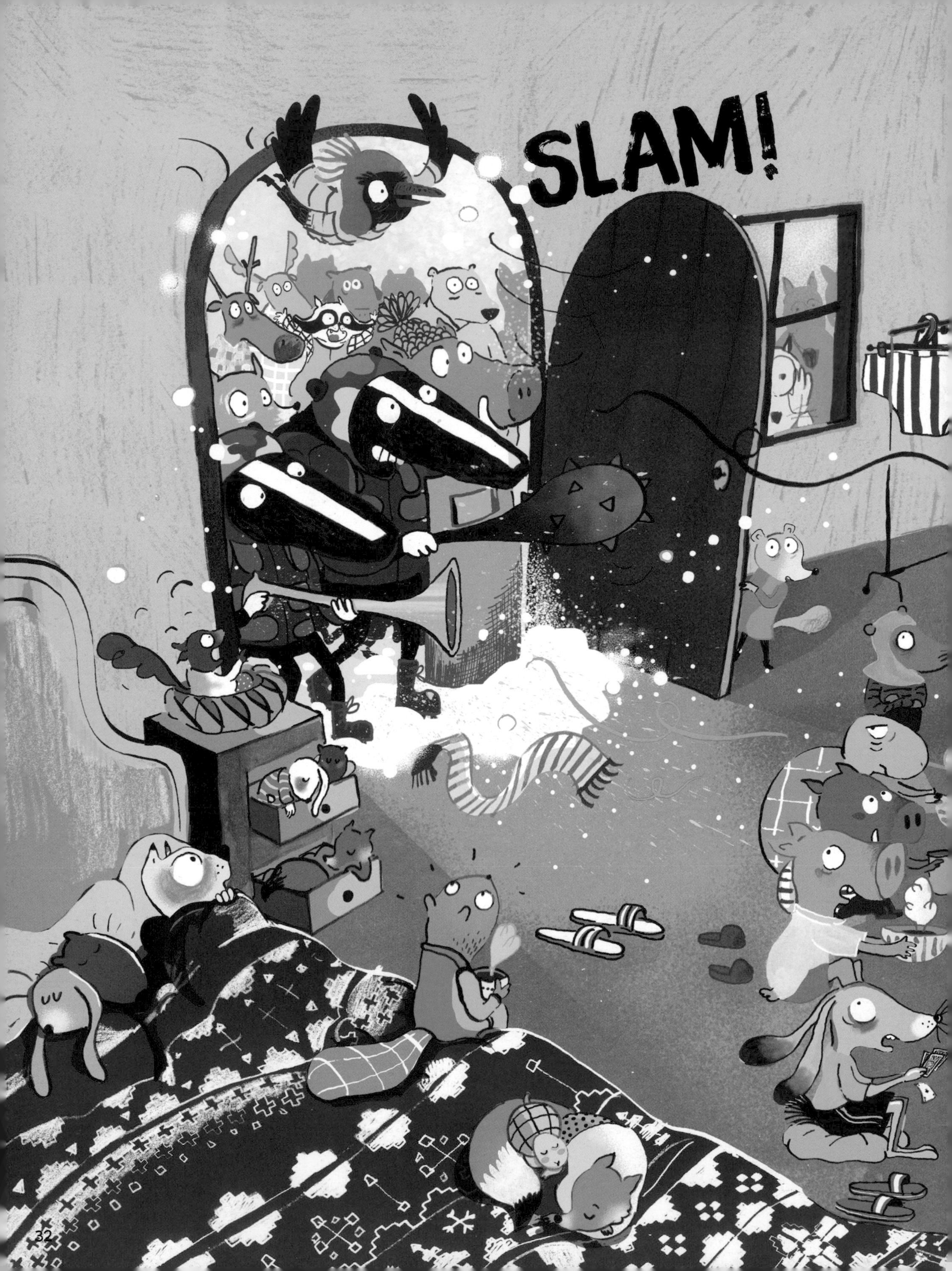
SLAM!

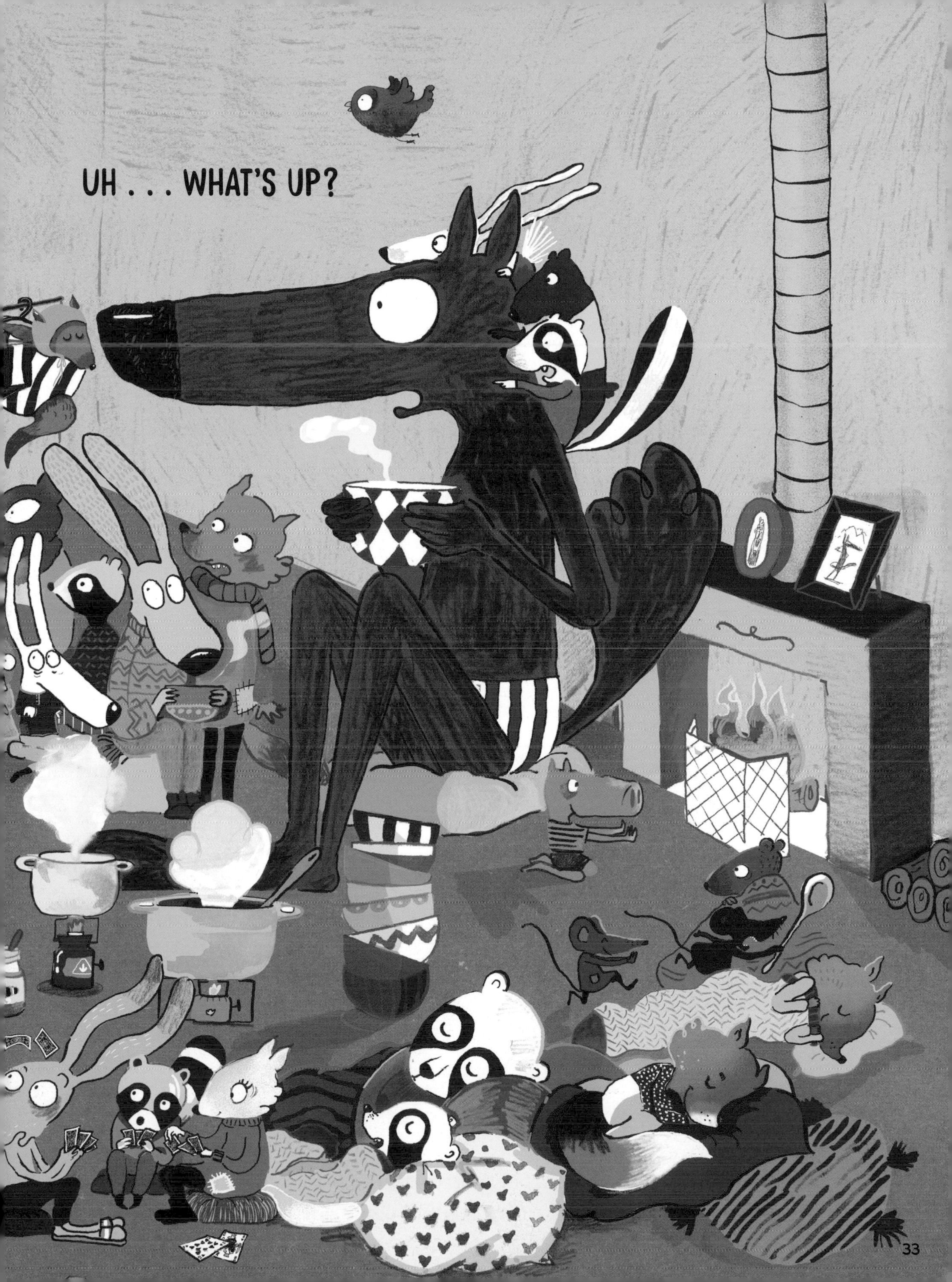
UH . . . WHAT'S UP?

UM . . . WELL, UH . . .

THE OTHER ANIMALS MADE US COME OVER HERE. CAUSE, WELL, YOU KEEP SAYING SOMETHING'S FREEZING.

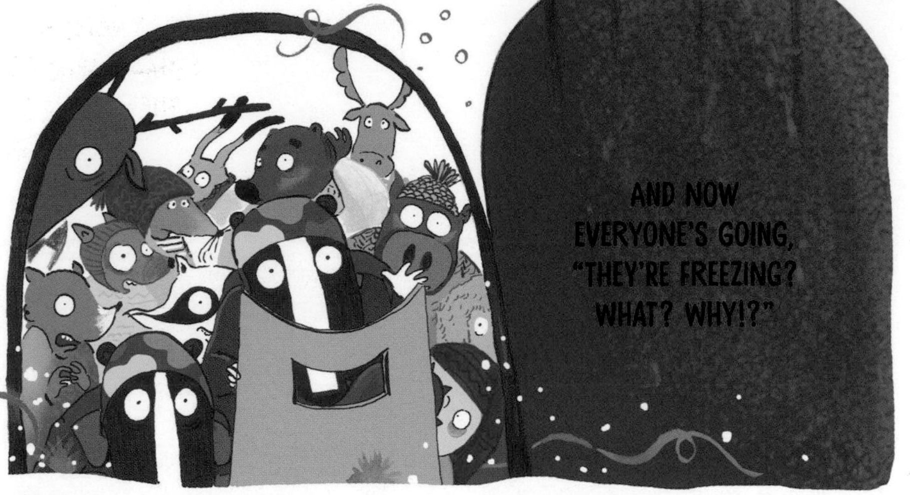
AND NOW EVERYONE'S GOING, "THEY'RE FREEZING? WHAT? WHY!?"

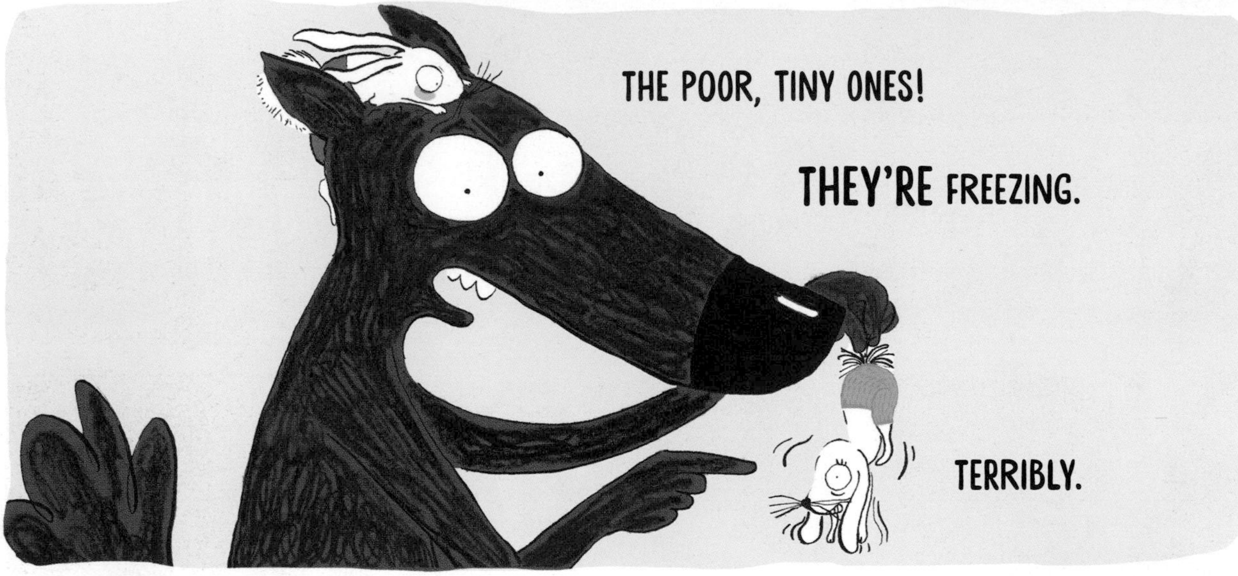
THE POOR, TINY ONES!
THEY'RE FREEZING.
TERRIBLY.

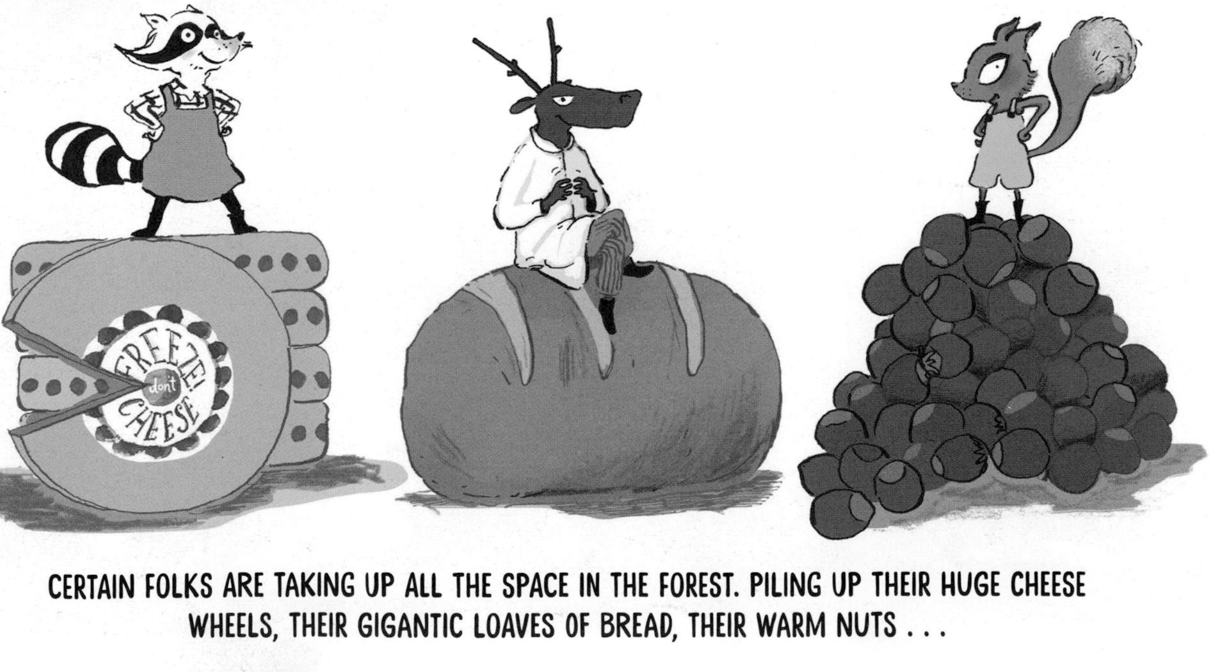
FREEZE! don't CHEESE

CERTAIN FOLKS ARE TAKING UP ALL THE SPACE IN THE FOREST. PILING UP THEIR HUGE CHEESE WHEELS, THEIR GIGANTIC LOAVES OF BREAD, THEIR WARM NUTS . . .

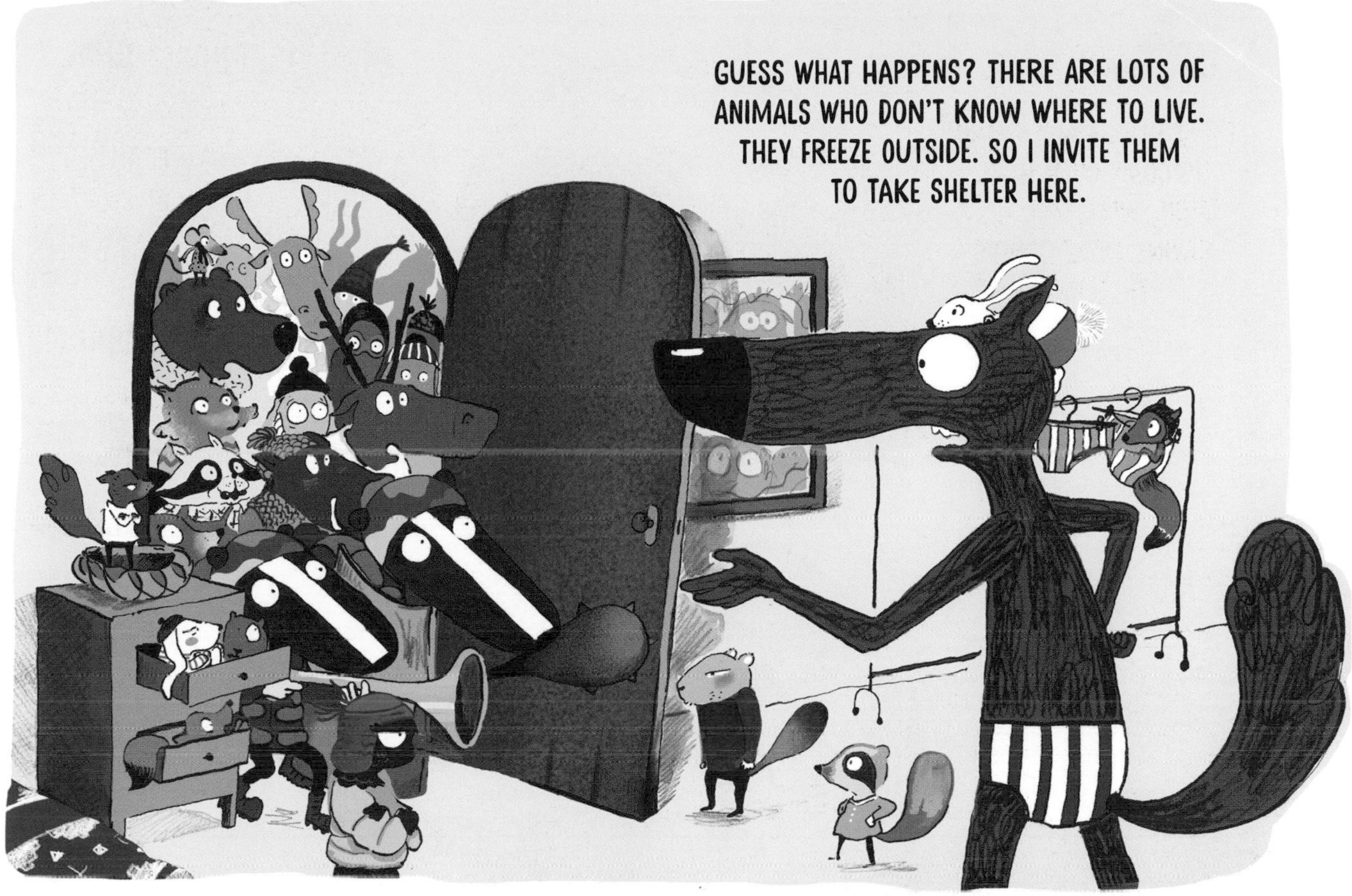
GUESS WHAT HAPPENS? THERE ARE LOTS OF ANIMALS WHO DON'T KNOW WHERE TO LIVE. THEY FREEZE OUTSIDE. SO I INVITE THEM TO TAKE SHELTER HERE.

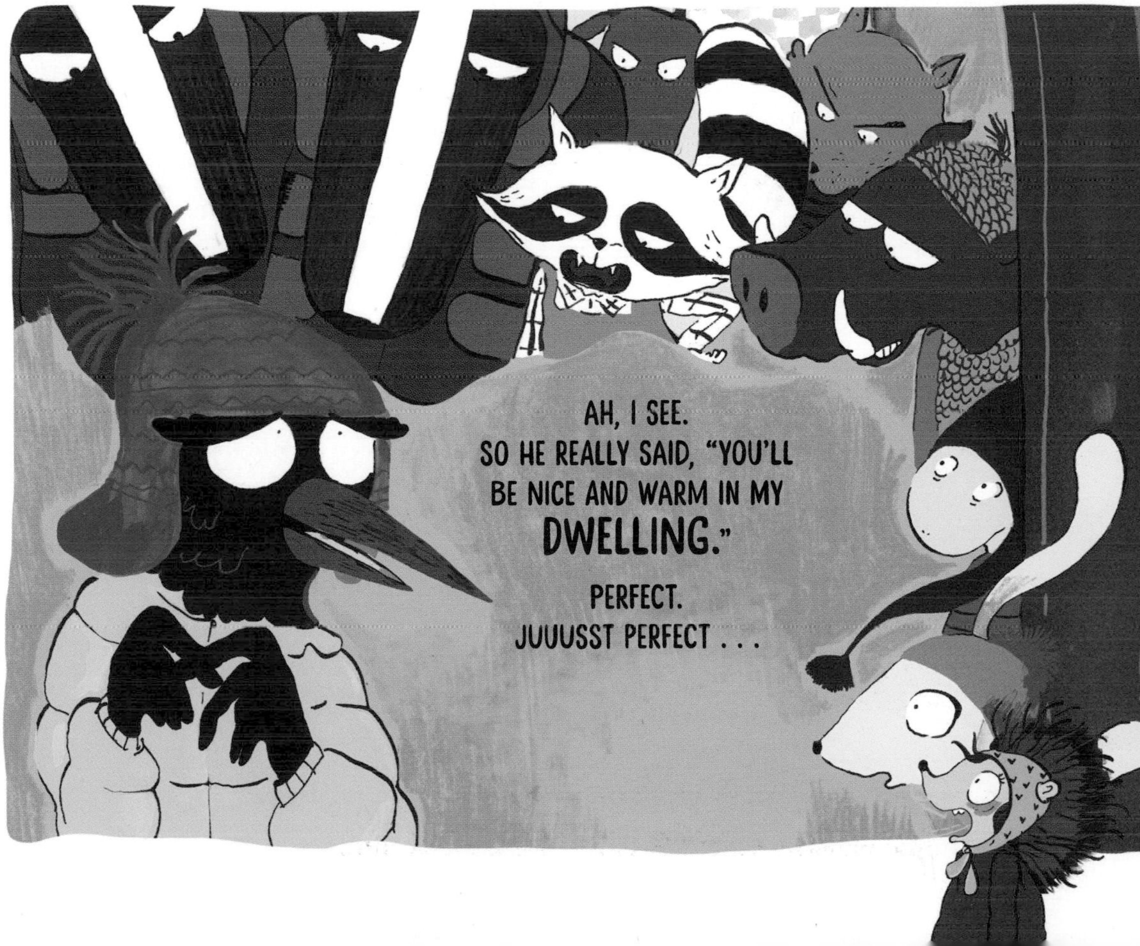
AH, I SEE.
SO HE REALLY SAID, "YOU'LL BE NICE AND WARM IN MY **DWELLING.**"
PERFECT.
JUUUSST PERFECT . . .

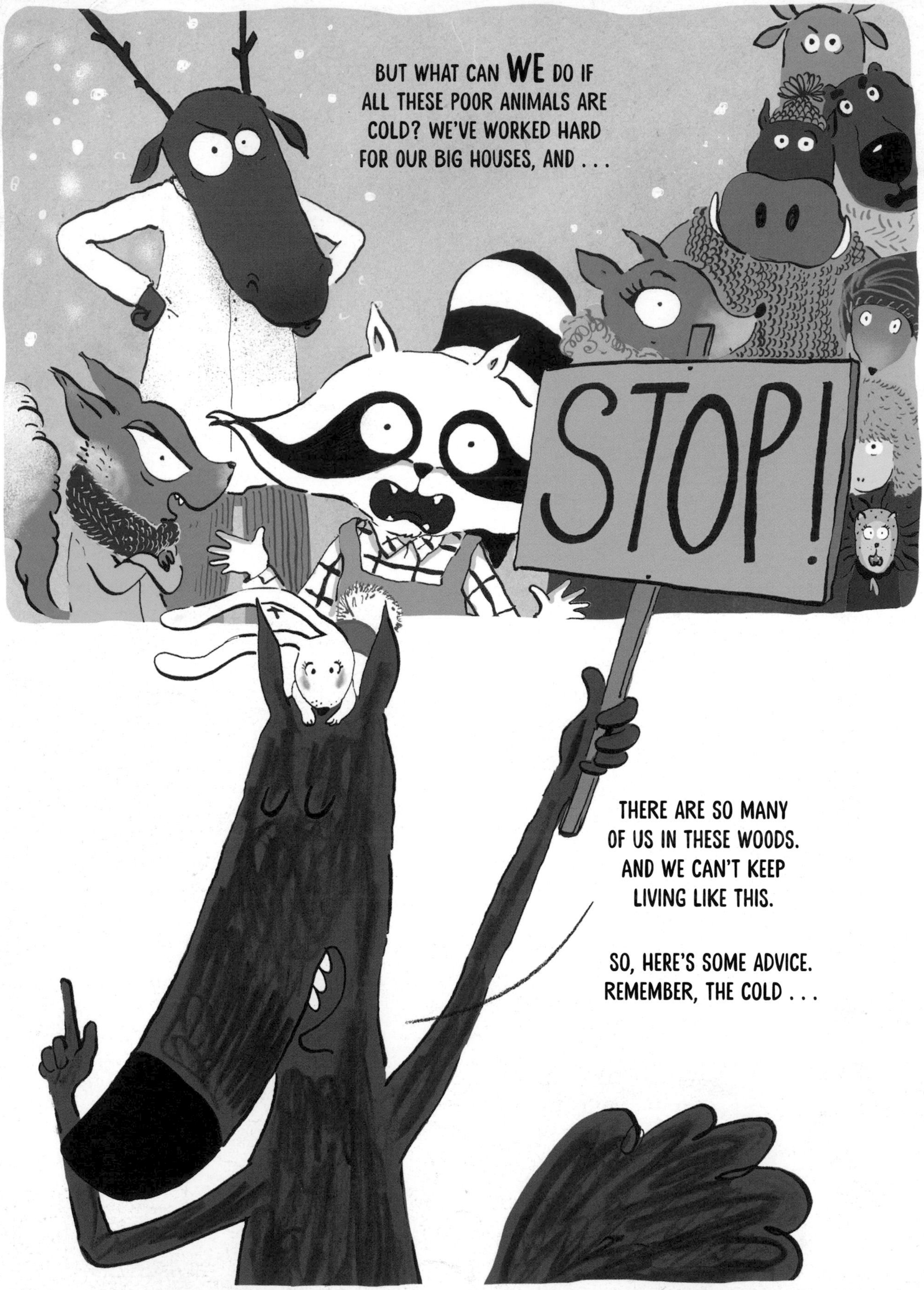
BUT WHAT CAN WE DO IF ALL THESE POOR ANIMALS ARE COLD? WE'VE WORKED HARD FOR OUR BIG HOUSES, AND . . .
STOP!
THERE ARE SO MANY OF US IN THESE WOODS. AND WE CAN'T KEEP LIVING LIKE THIS.
SO, HERE'S SOME ADVICE. REMEMBER, THE COLD . . .

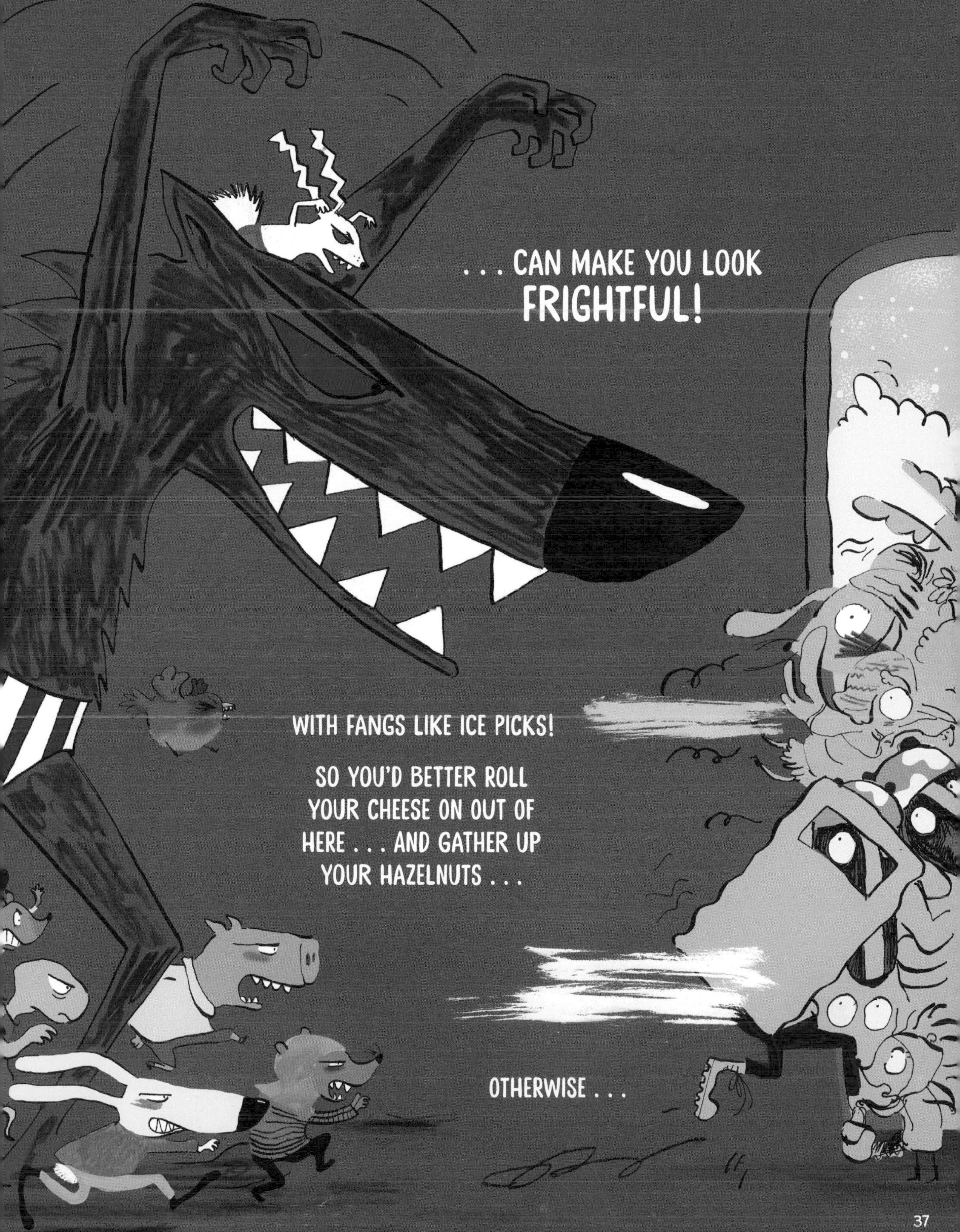

. . . CAN MAKE YOU LOOK **FRIGHTFUL!**

WITH FANGS LIKE ICE PICKS!

SO YOU'D BETTER ROLL YOUR CHEESE ON OUT OF HERE . . . AND GATHER UP YOUR HAZELNUTS . . .

OTHERWISE . . .

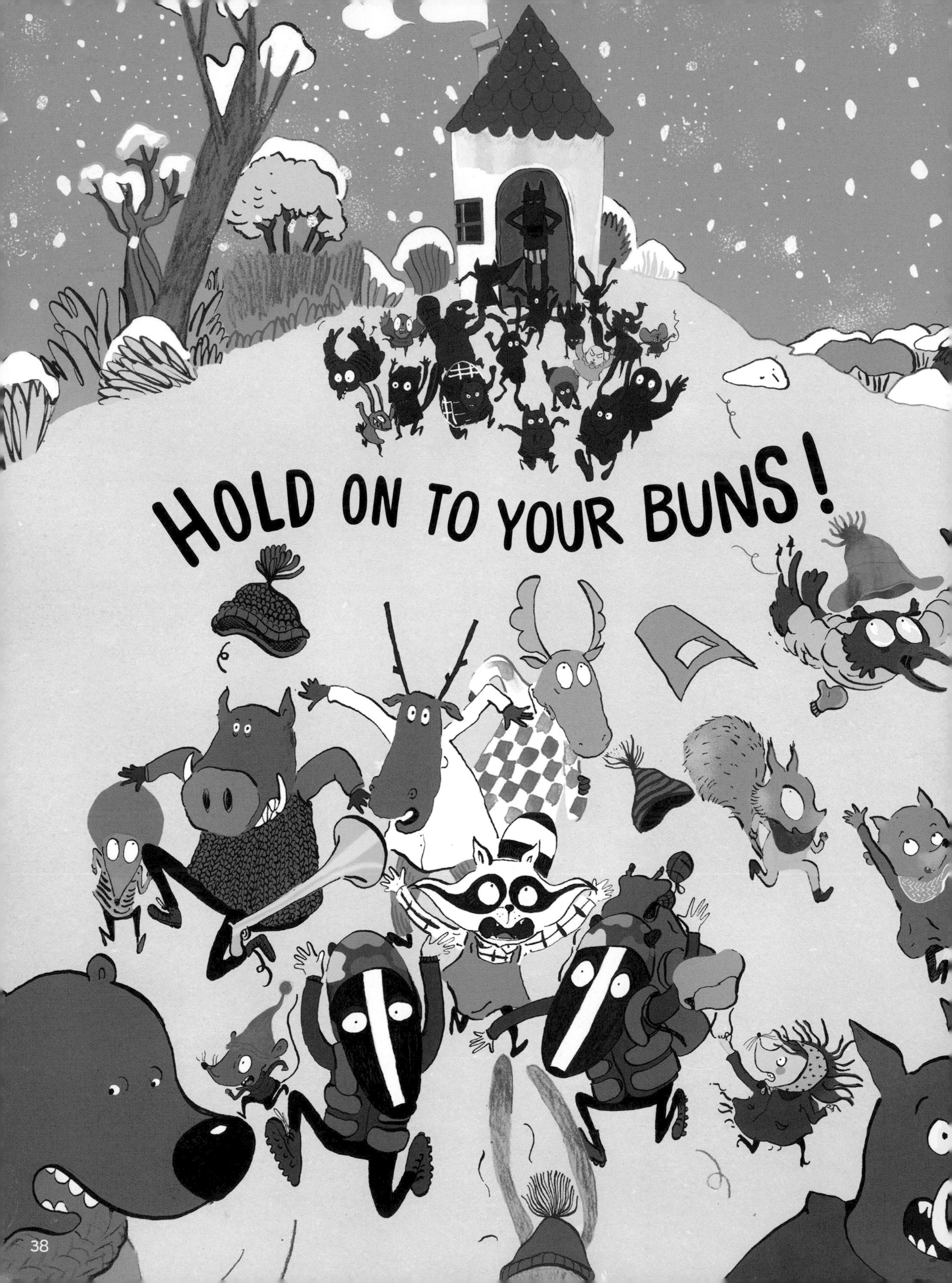
HOLD ON TO YOUR BUNS!

AFTER THIS WINTER MIX-UP, EVERYONE IN THE WOODS HAS TRIED A LITTLE HARDER TO BE KIND TO OTHERS. NOTHING'S PERFECT . . .

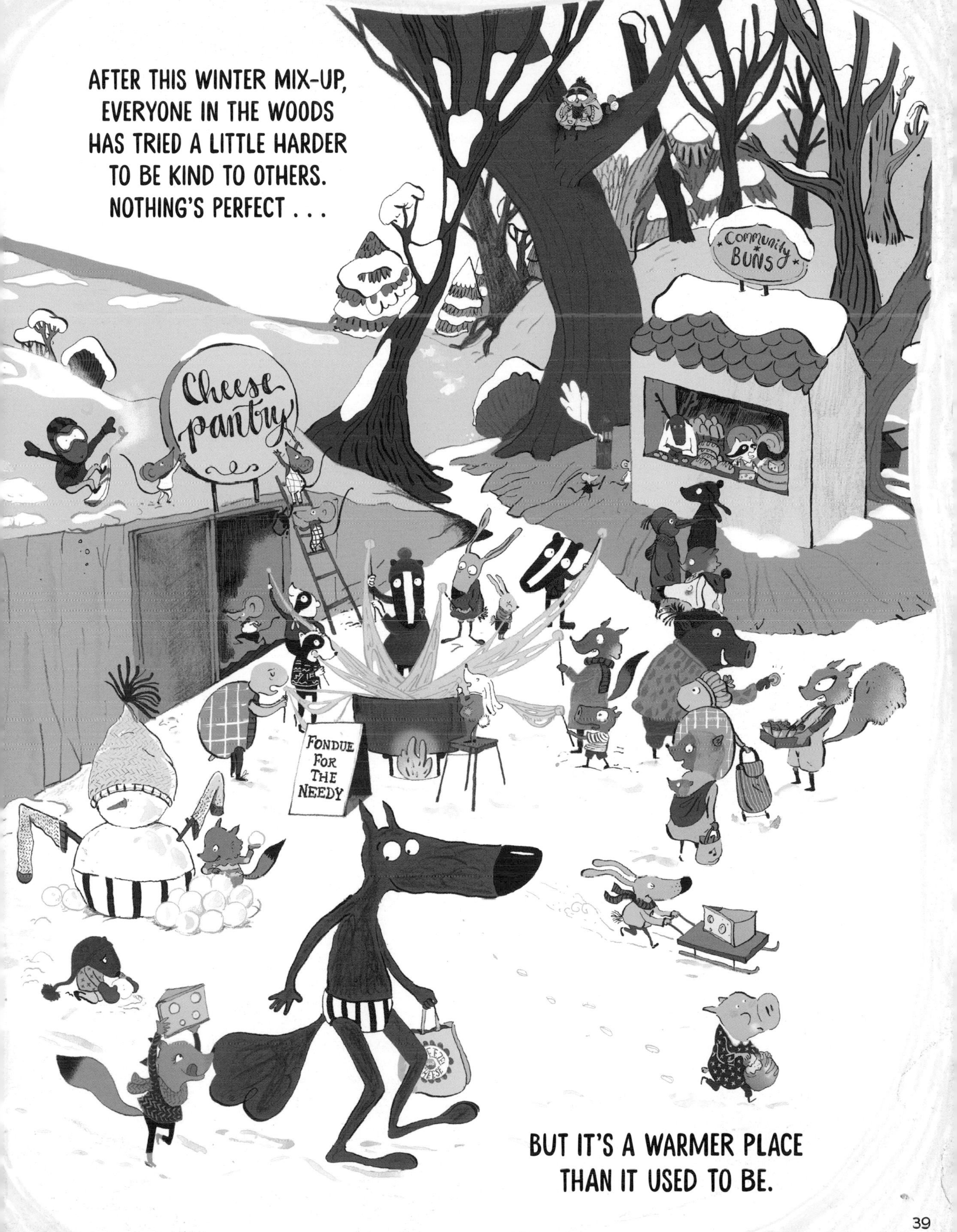
Cheese pantry
Community Buns
FONDUE FOR THE NEEDY

BUT IT'S A WARMER PLACE THAN IT USED TO BE.

ABOUT THE CREATORS

WILFRID LUPANO

Wilfrid Lupano was born in Nantes, in the west of France, and spent most of his childhood in the southwestern city of Pau, France. He spent his childhood reading through his parents' comic book collection and enjoying role-playing games. He studied literature and philosophy, receiving a degree in English, before he began to script comics. He has written numerous graphic novels for French readers, including the series *Les Vieux Fourneaux* (in English, *The Old Geezers*). With this series, Lupano and Paul Cauuet first developed the idea that would become *The Wolf in Underpants*. Lupano once again lives in Pau after spending several years in the city of Toulouse.

MAYANA ITOÏZ

Mayana Itoïz was born in the city of Bayonne, in the southwest of France, and studied at the institut supérieur des arts de Toulouse (School of Fine Arts in Toulouse), where she worked in many different mediums. In addition to being an illustrator and a cartoonist, she has taught art to high school students. She lives in the Pyrenees, near France's mountainous southern border, and splits her time between art, family, and travel.

PAUL CAUUET

Paul Cauuet was born in Toulouse and grew up in a family that encouraged his passion for drawing. He was also a fond reader of classic Franco-Belgian comics such as *Tintin* and *Asterix*. He studied at the University of Toulouse and went on to a career as a cartoonist. Cauuet and Wilfrid Lupano first collaborated on an outer-space comedy series before working together on *Les Vieux Fourneaux* (*The Old Geezers*).

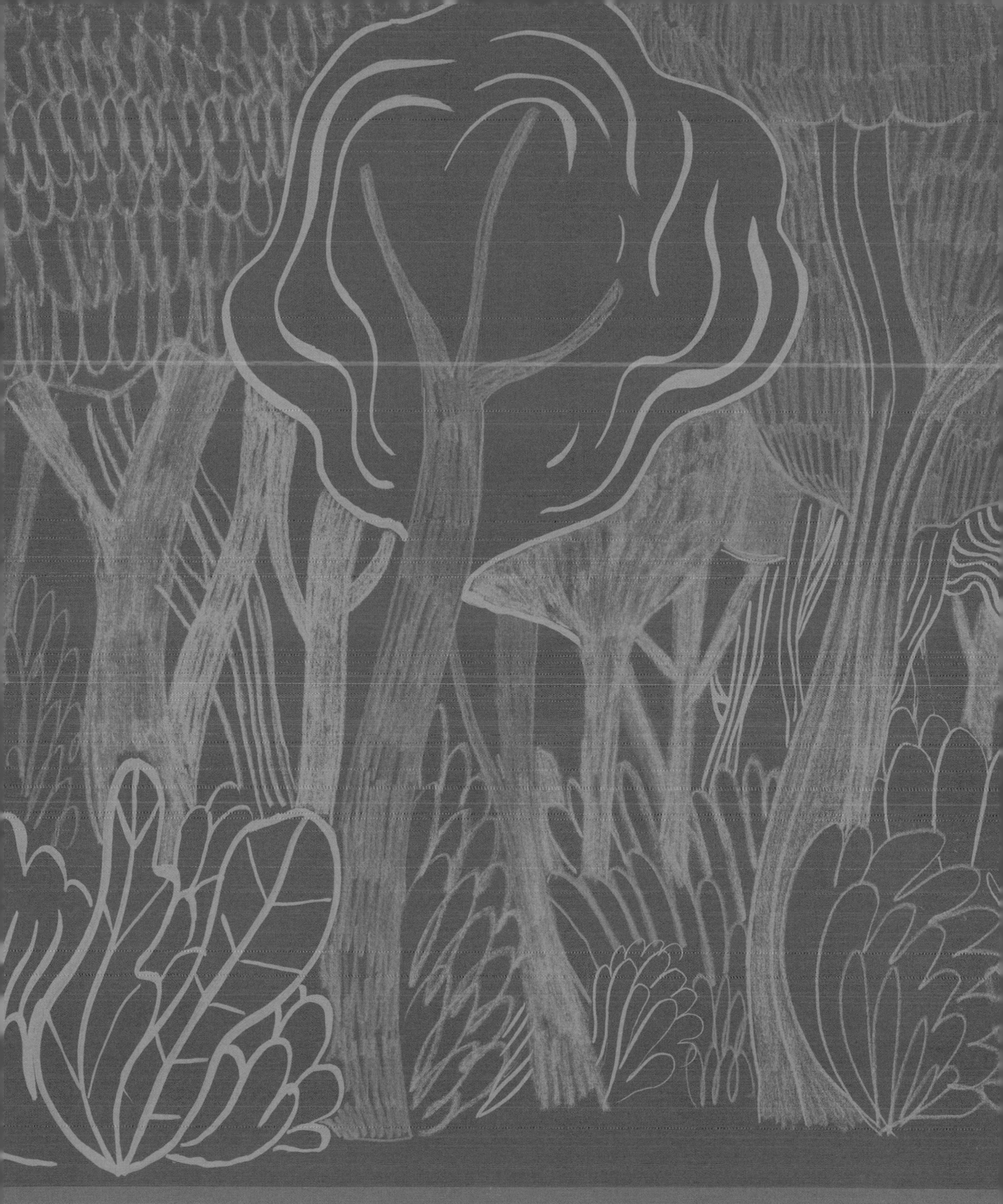

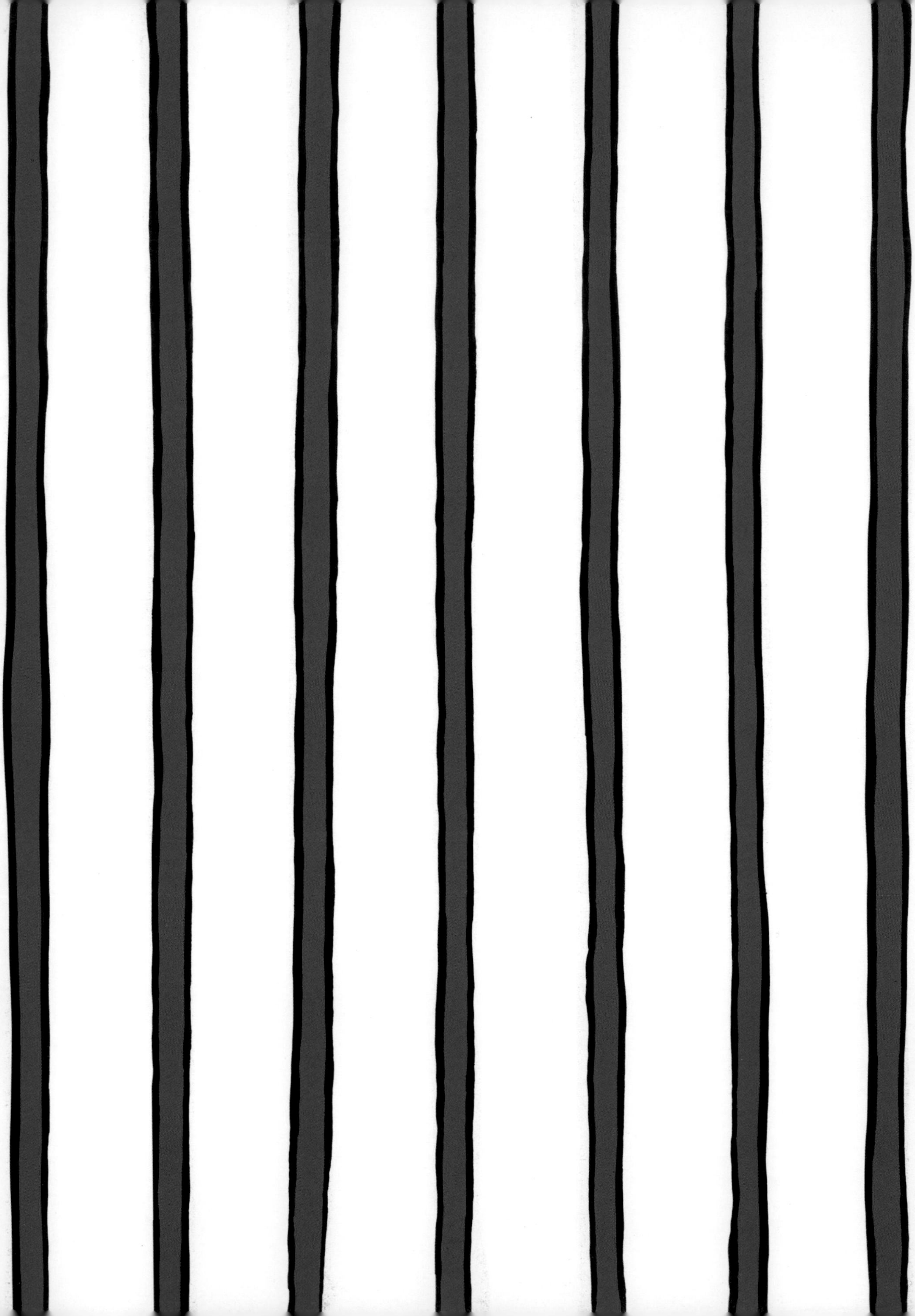

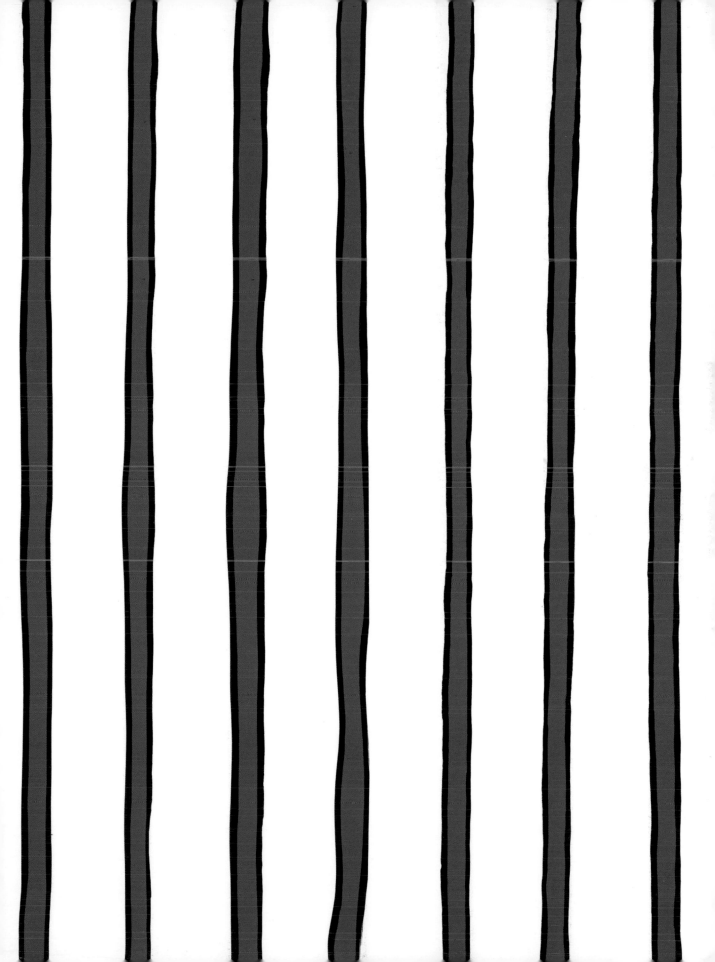